TO MY NIECE, ADDIE

THE CREEPS 2

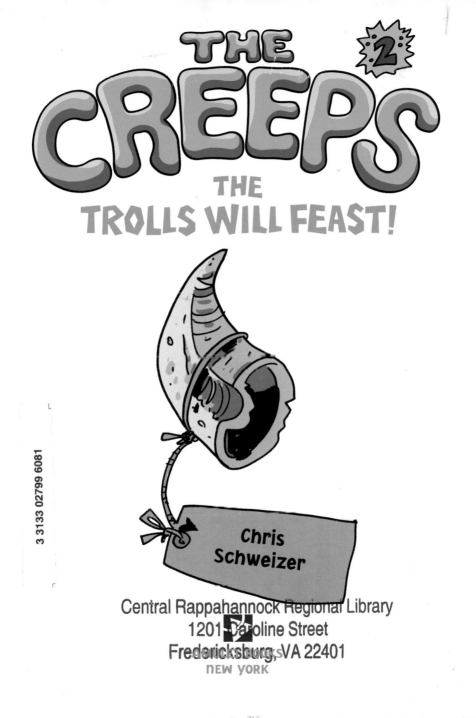

THE TROLLS WILL FEAST!

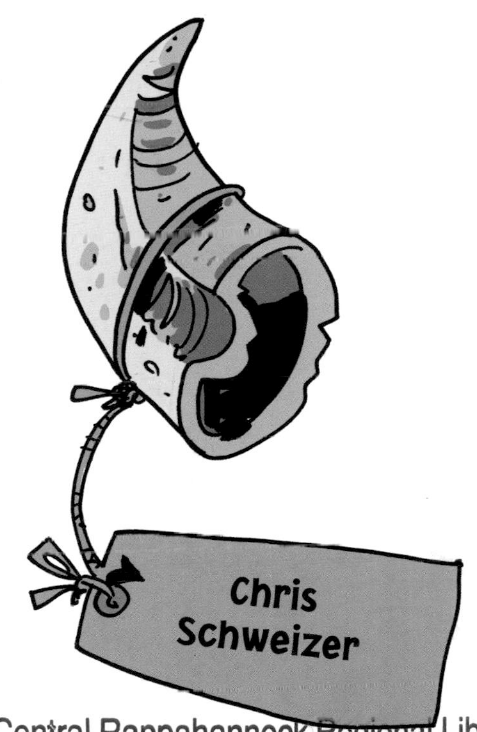

NEW YORK

PUBLISHER'S NOTE:
This is a work of fiction. Names, characters, places, and incidents are either the product of the author's imagination or used fictitiously, and any resemblance to actual persons, living or dead, business establishments, events, or locales is entirely coincidental.

Library of Congress Control Number: 2015944618

Hardcover ISBN: 978-1-4197-1882-3
Paperback ISBN: 978-1-4197-1883-0

Book design by Pamela Notarantonio
Color assistance by Liz Schweizer

Printed and bound in China
10 9 8 7 6 5 4 3 2 1

115 West 18th Street
New York, NY 10011
www.abramsbooks.com

PUMPKINS CO.
HARBOR AUTHORITY
WHERE ARE THOSE CREEPS, ANYWAY?

IT'S NOT ON **MY** FEED, IT'S NOT ON **MADISON'S**... IT'S JUST **GONE!**

MAYBE MADISON TOOK IT **DOWN.**
ROSARIO PLAP SINGING "NOTHING'S GONNA STOP ME FROM BEING A PRINCESS"?
THERE IS **NO WAY** MADISON WOULD TAKE THAT DOWN.
SLEDGE HAMME

IT'S THE FUNNIEST THING ANYONE HAS EVER SEEN!
THIS PLACE SMELLS **TRULY AWFUL.** WHAT WOULD YOU RATE IT? AN EIGHT?
DGE

IT'S A TEN.
THEY CAN'T **ALL** BE TENS!

THIS WHOLE **TOWN** IS A TEN. IT'S LIKE SOMEBODY STORED OLD MEAT IN AN ARMPIT.
AND RUBBED IT ON A SKUNK.
WHICH IS WHY WE NEED GOOD DATA TO PRESENT!

IF WE SAY THAT **EVERYTHING'S** A TEN, NO ONE WILL TAKE OUR STUDY SERIOUSLY.
OUR ASSIGNMENT IS TO FIND A WAY TO MAKE PUMPKINS COUNTY A BETTER PLACE TO LIVE. IF WE CAN MAKE OUR PROPOSAL LOOK **SCIENTIFIC...**
SLEDGE HAMMER

...THEN **MAYBE** WE CAN GET THE CITY COUNCIL TO ACTUALLY **DO** SOMETHING ABOUT THE INCREASING STINK ALL OVER TOWN.
WE'LL BE HEROES OF CIVIC ACTION!
SLEDGE HAMMER

THOSE CREEPS HAD **BETTER** BE ALMOST HERE.
I'M SICK OF WAITING. THIS PLACE IS GROSS.
SLEDGE HAMMER

TWO MORE MINUTES.
FINE.
IF I'VE GOT TO STAND AROUND, THOUGH...

...I'M GOING TO MAKE THIS PLACE AT LEAST A **LITTLE** MORE BREATHABLE.

WHAM!
MARY!
SLEDGE

KLONG

GRRRRRRRRRR
SLEDGE HAMMER

?

MARY?
UNGH

WHAT HIT ME?

...
I DON'T KNOW. I DIDN'T SEE ANYTHING.
SLEDGE HAMMER

MAYBE IT WAS A G-G-G-**GHOST!**

A **GHOST?** COME ON, ERNEST. NOW YOU SOUND LIKE THE **CREEPS.**
YEAH. YEAH. IT WAS PROBABLY JUST THE WIND.
JUST A SUPER FREAKY GROWLING WIND.

STILL...
I THINK WE'VE WAITED HERE LONG ENOUGH.
I'M WITH YOU THERE.
GRAB MY BODY SPRAY, WILL YOU?
SLEDGE HAMMER

NO PROBLEM.

YOINK
ERNEST!
AAAUGH!

NO NO NOOOOU...
CHOMP
W-
W-

CHOMP
CHOMP
CHOMP
GULP!
PTEWH!
THUNK!
WHUAAGH! WAUUAAAAAAGH!

...

ROARRRRR!

AAAAA!

GRAB!

AAAA
CHOMP

KANDICK CAN.CO
CHOMP
CHOMP
GULP!
RIVER
STOP

CAROL PONDICHERRY. KNOW-IT-ALL AND GENERAL RABBLE-ROUSER. THIS TOWN **WAS** A NICE, QUIET PLACE UNTIL **YOU** MOVED HERE.

NO, IT WASN'T! WEIRD STUFF HAPPENED HERE ALL THE TIME, IT'S JUST THAT NOBODY **DID** ANYTHING ABOUT IT!

JARVIS CLARK. FOUND WITH A SET OF LOCK PICKS, A GRAPPLING HOOK, A SILENT DOG WHISTLE, AND **SOME** KIND OF DEVICE THAT MAKES **PANTS** EXPLODE.

HEY, MY PANTS EJECTOR IS ONE HUNDRED PERCENT **LEGAL,** MAYBE!

EXIT

SNIFF

CLICK

DID YOU HEAR THAT, DEPUTY FINN? SHE **ADMITS** IT!

I HEARD.

ALL RIGHT, MAYHEW, TURN TO THE LEFT.
FINN! WHAT IS GOING ON HERE?
FINN

OH! SHERIFF. I, UH, I'VE ARRESTED THESE KIDS ON A CHARGE OF, UM...
TRESPASSING!
GRAND THEFT VIDEO!

...

OKAY, SO I'M NOT **EXACTLY** SURE WHAT TO CHARGE THEM WITH.

WILL **SOMEBODY** TELL ME WHAT THIS IS ALL ABOUT?
MADISON GRUSS SAW ROSARIO SINGING IN THE MUSIC ROOM BEFORE SCHOOL, AND RECORDED A **VIDEO** OF HER FROM THE HALLWAY.
I WAS...
IMPRESSED.
I'D NEVER SEEN SOMEONE **OUR AGE** SING A SONG FROM A **LITTLE KIDS'** MOVIE WITH SUCH...
ENTHUSIASM.

YEAH, **I** THOUGHT ROSARIO WAS SHY, BUT SHE WAS REALLY BELTING IT OUT, DANCING AROUND...
IT WAS **HILARIOUS!**
SHE **IS** SHY!

THAT'S WHY SHE WAS SINGING **BY HERSELF.**
SHE **WASN'T** BY HERSELF. SHE WAS AT **SCHOOL.**
AND IF SHE DIDN'T WANT ANYONE TO SEE HER...

...THEN **WHY** WAS SHE SINGING SO **LOUD?**
BECAUSE IT'S HER **FAVORITE SONG,** OF COURSE!
MITCHELL!

IT'S OKAY, ROSARIO!
I'M SURE IT'S **PERFECTLY NORMAL** TO LOVE **BABY SONGS!**
IT'S **NOT** A **BABY SONG!**
"NOTHING'S GONNA STOP ME FROM BEING A PRINCESS"?

THAT'S FROM **SLUMBERPUPPIES.**
I HAVEN'T WATCHED SLUMBERPUPPIES SINCE I WAS **FIVE.**
I DON'T SEE HOW ROSARIO SINGING...

...ENDS WITH YOU IN MY STATION.

MADISON PUT THE VIDEO UP ON **TATTLER** AND **SHARED** IT WITH HER FRIENDS.
EVERY KID IN SCHOOL!
IT'S **MY** VIDEO! I CAN PUT IT UP IF I WANT!
AND IT GOT LIKE A **GAZILLION** TATTLES!

EVERYONE IN TOWN WAS WATCHING IT!
IT'S TRUE, SIR. I WATCHED IT THIS MORNING. TWICE. IT WAS ABSOLUTELY **HILARIOUS.**

BUT THE **CREEPS** HACKED MY TATTLER ACCOUNT AND **DELETED** THE VIDEO!
THEY DELETED IT OFF **EVERYBODY'S** ACCOUNT!

THAT'S WHY THEY'RE HERE, SIR. ACCESSING MADISON GRUSS'S TATTLER ACCOUNT AND DELETING THE VIDEO.

I'M NOT GOING TO LET EVERYONE LAUGH AT MY FRIEND!
I'D DELETE IT AGAIN IN A **HEARTBEAT!**

I WANT THEM **LOCKED UP,** SHERIFF OBIE!
CYBER CRIMES!
I WANT **MADISON** LOCKED UP!
INVASION OF ROSARIO'S PRIVACY!
I WANT MY PANTS EJECTOR BACK!

ENOUGH.

...
...
...
...
...
...

THANK YOU.

NONE OF YOU HAS **TECHNICALLY** COMMITTED A CRIME. AT LEAST NOT ONE OVER WHICH **THIS** OFFICE HAS JURISDICTION.

YOU KIDS KNOW BETTER THAN TO FIDDLE AROUND ON OTHER FOLKS' COMPUTER ACCOUNTS. IT'S GOTTEN YOU INTO TROUBLE **BEFORE.**

JUST LIKE YOU'RE IN TROUBLE **NOW!**
AND **YOU** KIDS OUGHT TO KNOW BETTER THAN TO POST VIDEOS MAKING FUN OF YOUR CLASSMATES.

PRETTY SURE THAT PRINCIPAL GARISH HAS RULES ABOUT BULLYING.
IT WASN'T BULLYING!

I **WROTE** ON THE VIDEO "LISTEN TO ROSARIO SING THIS BABY SONG WITH ALL HER HEART. SHE'S SO BRAVE TO NOT CARE WHAT PEOPLE THINK!"

I SAID SHE WAS BRAVE! **COMPLIMENTS** AREN'T **BULLYING.**
SHERIFF, I AIN'T GOT TIME FOR THIS.

IF YOU'RE GONNA QUESTION ME, THEN QUESTION ME...

...OTHERWISE, LET ME GET BACK TO WORK.
DEPUTY FINN, WE GOT A TIP THAT **JOCK BROGGLIN** HERE HAS BEEN SMUGGLING **CONTRABAND** INTO TOWN ON HIS BOAT.
GET RID OF THESE KIDS. WE'VE GOT **REAL** POLICE-WORK TO DO.

I'D LIKE MY PANTS EJECTOR BACK, PLEASE.

I CAN'T BELIEVE HE KEPT MY LOCK PICKS!
I CAN'T BELIEVE I GOT A MUG SHOT!

WE'RE GOING TO BE STUCK DOING THE WHOLE STUDY ON OUR OWN, I BET!

I DON'T SEE ANYBODY.
IF THEY'RE NOT HERE NOW, THEY **WERE.** ONE OF THE MESSAGES MARY SENT HAS A PHOTO OF ERNEST IN THIS ALLEY, LOOKING IMPATIENT.
YUCK! HE SURE PICKED A GOOD PLACE FOR US TO START, DIDN'T HE?
IT **DOES** SMELL BAD.

WHICH IS A GOOD THING, CONSIDERING OUR OBJECTIVE!
I THOUGHT YOU WERE EMBARRASSED ABOUT OUR GROUP DOING THE STINK STUDY. WHY THE ABOUT-FACE?
I'D RATHER BE THOUGHT OF AS ONE OF THE STINK-STUDY KIDS THAN AS THE GIRL IN THE PRINCESS VIDEO.
EVERYONE BRING THE SCALE SHEET THAT ERNEST SENT OUT?
ERNEST SLEDGE
STINK SCALE
THIS PLACE HAS GOT TO BE A TEN ON THE ERNEST SLEDGE STINK SCALE.
THE ALLEY BEHIND VENABLE'S PIZZA IS WAY SMELLIER.
GUYS, I THINK SOMETHING HAPPENED TO ERNEST AND MARY.
SOMETHING BAD.
OKAY, WE HAVE A HABIT OF JUMPING TO CONCLUSIONS, SO LET'S JUST TAKE A MINUTE.
JUST BECAUSE WE FOUND ERNEST'S EMPTY SHOE COVERED IN MUCUS DOESN'T MEAN THAT—
HE WAS EATEN BY A MONSTER!
WE DON'T KNOW THAT.
YEAH...
...WE DO.

...
THAT'S MARY GARRIGAN'S PHONE.
GARRIGAN WOULD **NEVER LEAVE** IT SOMEWHERE.
SO THEY WERE **BOTH** EATEN BY A MONSTER!

WE'RE NEAR THE WATER. COULD IT HAVE BEEN ONE OF THOSE **CATFISH PEOPLE** THAT MITCHELL'S ALWAYS TALKING ABOUT?
THIS IS THE **RIVER.** THE CATFISH PEOPLE LIVE IN THE **LAKE.**

I WROTE A WHOLE BIG SECTION ABOUT THEM IN THE ***CREATURE COMPENDIUM.*** YOU GUYS REALLY OUGHT TO READ THE UPDATES.
HEY, CAROL, IS THIS A **CLUE?**

"LAVENDER DREAM" BODY SPRAY? NO, I THINK IT'S JUST TRASH.
LAVENDER DREAM?!

YOU CAN'T GET THAT AROUND HERE! IT'S SUPPOSED TO SMELL **HEAVENLY!**

IS THERE ANY LEFT IN IT, JARVIS?
I'LL CHECK.

JARVIS, YOU'RE FLYING!

HOLD ON, BEST BUDDY O' MINE, **I'LL** GET YOU DOWN!

I'M NOT FLYING!

HOP HOP

SOMETHING JUST BIT DOWN ON MY HELMET!
CRNCH
CRCH

HANG ON, JARVIS!

THUD
ROARR!

IT STOPPED BITING, BUT IT'S STILL GOT MY PANT LEG!
USE YOUR PANTS EJECTOR, JARVIS!

OH, YEAH!
CLICK

BOOM!

ROAARR!
GO, GO, GO!
SMASH
DON'T SLOW DOWN, I'M FIIIIIIINE!
SMASH

THUTHUMP
OOF!
THIS WAY!

WHAT ARE WE DOING?
GOING FAST!

BUT THE RIVERFRONT IS A DEAD END!
YEAH, BUT THE OTHER WAY IS UPHILL!

TURN! THE BOAT RAMP!
ON IT!

LOOK OUT!

CRASH!

TOMPKINS CO.
HARBOR AUTHORITY
AARGH!

EVERYBODY OKAY DOWN THERE?
ARE YOU KIDS **CRAZY?!**

DO YOU **KNOW** HOW **BADLY** YOU COULD GET **HURT** BY **NOT WATCHING WHERE YOU'RE GOING?!**

SORRY, DEPUTY FINN! WE WERE ESCAPING FROM A MONSTER!

FINN

WE **WERE!** IT WAS...
UM...
INVISIBLE.

YOU RECONSIDERING LETTING ME LOCK THEM UP, SHERIFF?
YEP.

LUCKY FOR **THEM,** OUR TIME IS CURRENTLY OCCUPIED WITH SEARCHIN' JOCK BROGGLIN'S **BOAT.**
YOU **AIN'T** GONNA FIND NUTHIN' **ILLEGAL.**

NOW YOU KIDS GET ON HOME. WE'VE ABOUT HAD OUR FILL OF YOU FOR ONE DAY.

AND JARVIS?
YES, SHERIFF?

PUT ON SOME PANTS, SON.
YES, SIR!

LET US IN, GERARD!

NO CAN DO, LITTLE BRO.
MOM SAID **NO COMPANY.** MY HANDS ARE TIED.
SHE ONLY SAID THAT BECAUSE SHE DIDN'T WANT **YOU** TO HAVE CLARA OVER WHILE NO ONE WAS HOME!
HE ♥ LOOOOVES HER!
WHO'S CLARA?
GERARD'S GIRLFRIEND.
MOM'S RULES AFFECT US **ALL,** YOUNG MITCHELL.
I SUGGEST THAT **YOU** CAMPAIGN ON OUR BEHALF TO HAVE THE RULES CHANGED SO WE CAN BOTH ACT THE HOST WHENEVER IT SUITS US. MAYBE **YOU'LL** HAVE MORE LUCK CONVINCING MOM THAN I DID.
BUT WE NEED TO GET MY MONSTER BOOKS, AND JARVIS NEEDS HIS EMERGENCY BACKUP PANTS!
YOU HAVE A PAIR OF EMERGENCY PANTS HERE?
BABY, I GOT EMERGENCY PANTS STASHED **ALL OVER TOWN!**
THE ONES **HERE** ARE TAPED TO THE UNDERSIDE OF THE PIANO BENCH.
OKAAAAY.
I'LL GRAB THEM FOR YOU.
YOU'RE WELCOME TO COME IN, LITTLE BRO, BUT YOUR PALS SHAN'T JOIN YOU.
GO ON, MITCHELL. AT LEAST GRAB THE BOOK WE NEED.
I DON'T **KNOW** WHAT BOOK WE NEED, BECAUSE I DON'T KNOW WHAT KIND OF **MONSTER** WE JUST ENCOUNTERED!
WELL, WE KNOW IT WAS **INVISIBLE.** THAT NARROWS IT DOWN.
OR THAT IT **FLIES** AND WAS SO **SMALL** THAT WE COULDN'T **SEE** IT.
LIKE A SUPER-STRONG **BUG.**
IT **WASN'T** SMALL. IT CHOMPED DOWN ON MY **HELMET,** REMEMBER? IT SLOBBERED **ALL OVER ME!**

HEY, THAT'S RIGHT! IT **DID** BITE YOUR HELMET.

WE CAN EXAMINE IT FOR CLUES!
HEY!

HMM... THAT'S WEIRD. IT'S LIKE THERE'S SOME KIND OF **FORCE BUBBLE** AROUND THE DENT FROM THE BITE.

MITCHELL, EVER HEARD OF A MONSTER WHOSE **BITE MARKS** BECOME **FORCE FIELDS?**
NOPE.

POP!
BUT AN INVISIBLE **MONSTER** MIGHT LEAVE AN INVISIBLE **TOOTH.**
OH.
YEAH.

I'VE GOT AN IDEA!
JARVIS, I NEED YOU TO DRAW.
GLAD TO.

HERE, TOUCH THIS AND DRAW WHAT YOU FEEL, OKAY?

CAN DO, OL' PAL.

HERE Y'GO, MITCHELL.
HMMM...

...IT LOOKS LIKE A TUSK.
SO WHAT'S **INVISIBLE** AND HAS **TUSKS?**

AN ENCHANTED JAVALINA!
A WALRUS WITH A CLOAKING DEVICE!

I THINK IT'S A **TROLL.**

TROLLS ARE **INVISIBLE?**
WELL, **WE'RE** NOT ABLE TO **SEE** THEM. WHICH ISN'T EXACTLY THE SAME THING.
THROW ME THOSE PANTS, GERARD!

THERE YOU GO, CHAMP!
THANKS!

YOU'RE NOT PUTTING THEM ON?
I HAVE TO CONNECT THE EJECTOR PROPELLENTS TO THE BUCKLE FIRST.
OKAY, GUYS...

...WHAT KIND OF TROUBLE ARE YOU GETTING UP TO?
SOMETHING ATE OUR CLASSMATES. MITCHELL THINKS IT MIGHT BE A **TROLL.**

AW, COME ON, GUYS. EVERY TIME YOU SHOUT "MONSTER" THE WHOLE TOWN GETS MAD AT YOU. JUST **BE COOL.**

YOU GUYS MIGHT BE A LITTLE WEIRD AND STUFF, BUT YOU'RE ALL RIGHT.
JUST TONE DOWN THE MONSTER STUFF. IT BUMS ME OUT THAT EVERYONE THINKS OF YOU GUYS AS, WELL...

...YOU KNOW...
CREEPS.
REAL NICE, GERARD.
EVERYONE TREATS **US** LIKE DIRT, AND **WE'RE** THE ONES WHO NEED TO CHANGE?

I'M NOT SAYING THAT YOU **DESERVE** TO BE PICKED ON. I'M JUST SAYING THAT YOU MAKE YOURSELVES REALLY EASY TARGETS.

YOU CAN **LIKE** STUFF THAT'S UNUSUAL...
I MEAN, **I'M** BONKERS FOR FARM-CRAFTED ARTISANAL CHEESES...
...BUT, YOU KNOW, PLAY IT CLOSE TO THE VEST.

SO PRETEND THAT WE DON'T CARE ABOUT THE STUFF WE CARE ABOUT?
EXACTLY!

PASSION IS A LUXURY AFFORDED LITTLE KIDS AND GROWN-UPS.
THE WATERS OF ADOLESCENT SOCIAL STANDING ARE CHOPPY, MY LITTLE FRIENDS, AND IT HELPS TO HAVE...
UM...

I DON'T KNOW, A BOAT OR SOMETHING?
I KIND OF LOST THE METAPHOR, BUT IF PEOPLE THINK THAT **YOU'RE** MORE OR LESS LIKE **THEM,** THEN THEY'LL **LIKE** YOU MORE.

I DON'T CARE ABOUT BEING LIKED BY PEOPLE SO SHALLOW THAT THEY CAN'T HANDLE ANYONE WHO ACTS DIFFERENT.
I DO.

ANYWAY, MITCHELL'S THE ONE WHO LIKES MONSTERS. I DON'T GIVE TWO FIGS ABOUT THEM. BUT I'M GOOD AT SOLVING MYSTERIES, AND THIS TOWN HAS LOTS OF THEM!
YEAH, AND EVERY TIME YOU "SOLVE" ONE, IT CAUSES PROBLEMS!

LIKE THAT GREAT SUSHI PLACE THAT GOT SHUT DOWN THANKS TO YOUR "INVESTIGATING."
THEIR UNAGI ROLLS WERE TURNING PEOPLE INTO EEL MUTANTS!

WISH I GOT TO BE AN EEL MUTANT.
OKAY, HERE'S WHAT I'VE GOT ON TROLLS.
ONLY TWO BOOKS? USUALLY WE HAVE TO LIMIT YOU TO HALF A DOZEN!

MOST REPUTABLE TROLL STUDIES ARE IN NORWEGIAN. THIS IS THE ONLY ENGLISH STUFF I'VE GOT.
SO YOU REALLY SAW A TROLL?

WELL, WE DIDN'T SEE IT, EXACTLY.
TROLLS ARE TECHNICALLY A KIND OF FAIRY. NOT THE KIND OF FAIRY THAT WE THINK OF. LIKE, NOT A TINY PERSON WITH DRAGONFLY WINGS OR WHATEVER...
...BUT THE OLD MEANING OF FAIRY.
FAIR FOLK.
MAGICAL CREATURES WITH THEIR OWN WORLD WHO CAN ENTER THIS ONE AND CAUSE TROUBLE.

FAIR FOLK ALWAYS RESIDE PARTIALLY IN THE WORLD OF MAGIC, AND AS SUCH CAN'T BE SEEN BY HUMAN MORTALS WITHOUT THE AID OF SPELLS OR HERBS OR SOMETHING TO PIERCE THE VEIL BETWEEN THE TWO PLANES OF EXISTENCE.

SO...
NO.

-SIGH-
YOU KIDS DO YOUR THING, I GUESS.
FAIRIES, MITCHELL? FAIRIES?
I'D LOVE TO SEE A REAL FAIRY!
WELL, THESE FAIRIES ARE GIANT, MEAN, AND STINKY.

RESEARCH TIME!
THUD

LET'S READ THROUGH TOGETHER, SHALL WE?

SO WE'RE PROBABLY NOT LOOKING AT ONE TROLL, BUT A LOT OF THEM.
THEY LIVE IN TRIBES OR CLANS. THEY EVEN HIBERNATE COMMUNALLY.
Slumb'r lengthy is the beasts' respite
With men their gullets swell'd to stem their
Wherefore they gorge not outside single night
One wey o'erhead their hung'r for to slake

YEAH, I THINK SO. BUT I HAVEN'T BEEN ABLE TO FIGURE OUT WHAT THE VERSE UNDER THE ILLUSTRATION MEANS.

ANY GUESSES?

OCULUS

CANTATIS

kin, find not thyself at trol àback
Its residency pungency forewarned
though you in glimpses stolen shan't find lack
Thy lamps awash'd in milk of nanny horn'd

NOPE. NO GUESSES.
WHAT DOES THIS PART ABOUT **LAMPS** MEAN?

"THY LAMPS AWASH'D IN MILK OF NANNY HORN'D."
MAYBE IF WE PUT A SPECIAL KIND OF MILK ON AN OLD LAMP, LIKE AN OIL LAMP, MAYBE THE LIGHT SHINING OUT WOULD SHOW THE TROLLS?

OR MAYBE YOU'RE SUPPOSED TO PUT THE MILK **IN** THE LAMP, INSTEAD OF **OIL.**
THERE'S AN OLD OIL LAMP IN OUR **SHED!**
EASY, GUYS...

LIKE YOU SAID, A "SPECIAL KIND" OF MILK. A "NANNY" MIGHT MEAN, LIKE, A NURSEMAID, BUT **I** DON'T **KNOW** ANY NURSEMAIDS.
MUCH LESS ANY THAT HAVE HORNS.

WHAT HAS HORNS? A SATYR?
I THINK SATYRS ARE MALE. YOU CAN'T MILK MALES.
I'M NOT MILKING **ANYTHING.**

I THINK IT'S A DEAD END CLUE, GUYS. IT WAS WRITTEN HUNDREDS OF YEARS AGO. FOR ALL WE KNOW, A "NANNY HORN'D" COULD BE A TYPE OF MILK BOTTLE, OR A TOWN, OR WHO KNOWS WHAT. WE GOT NUTHIN.'

COME ON, MITCHELL. IF I KNOW YOU, THEN YOU'VE **PORED** OVER THIS BOOK. YOU **MUST** HAVE FOUND SOME OTHER CLUES OR **SOMETHING** THAT CAN HELP!
I'VE DONE MY BEST, CAROL, BUT I DON'T UNDERSTAND MUCH OF THE WRITING, AND MOST OF THE ILLUSTRATIONS ARE EITHER PICTURES OF TROLLS SLEEPING OR DIAGRAMS OF THEIR DIGESTIVE SYSTEMS.
EWW!

SO WE COULDN'T FIGURE OUT THE BIT ABOUT HOW TO **SEE** THEM...
...IS THERE ANYTHING IN THE BOOK ABOUT HOW TO **STOP** THEM?

MITCHELL...
OKAY, MAYBE THERE'S **SOMETHING.**

BUT I THINK IT MIGHT BE ABOUT HOW TO **KILL** TROLLS. **I** DON'T WANT TO KILL **ANYTHING.**
FOR ALL WE KNOW, THEY'RE GENTLE AT HEART AND JUST WANT TO BE LEFT ALONE.

THEY ATE MARY AND ERNEST.
THAT DOESN'T SAY "GENTLE" TO **ME.**
GOOD POINT.
OKAY, HERE IN THE BACK. I COULDN'T FIGURE THIS SECTION OUT, EITHER.

YEP. THAT TROLL LOOKS DEADER THAN A DOORNAIL.
If seek ye monsters' end as end betide
A trill from passion's fountainhead declare
Its heart untanned, a pole against its hide
For strain believed is more than it can bear
THIS VERSE DOESN'T MAKE ANY MORE SENSE THAN THE **OTHER** ONE.
HERE!

WE PUT, UM, A POLE AGAINST ITS HIDE.
ACTUALLY, I THINK IN **THIS** CASE THE WORD "POLE" MEANS "OPPOSITE."
ITS **HEART** ISN'T HARD LIKE ITS **HIDE.**

HOW ARE WE SUPPOSED TO GET THROUGH TO ITS VULNERABLE HEART IF ITS HIDE IS HARD?
I DON'T KNOW! I **SAID** I COULDN'T MAKE HEADS OR TAILS OF THIS.

YOU BROUGHT OUT TWO BOOKS. IS THE OTHER ONE EASIER TO READ?
IT'S EASIER, BUT IT'S NOT EXACTLY HELPFUL. IT DOESN'T TELL YOU MUCH ABOUT TROLLS **OR** HOW TO FIGHT THEM.
IT'S MORE LIKE, I DON'T KNOW, WEIRD CONSPIRACY THEORIES. LIKE THAT TROLLS ARE RESPONSIBLE FOR THE CUBAN MISSILE CRISIS AND STUFF.

I ONLY READ A COUPLE CHAPTERS OF IT. I THINK WHOEVER WROTE IT IS PROBABLY CRAZY.
I ONLY BROUGHT IT OUTSIDE BECAUSE I FELT KIND OF LIKE A CHUMP HAVING ONLY ONE GOOD TROLL BOOK.

YOU'RE NOT A CHUMP, MITCHELL! YOU'RE THE SMARTEST GUY I KNOW!
SWEET POTATO PUMPKIN PIE!
CHECK OUT WHO THE **AUTHOR** IS!

the TROLL PLOT

GUESS WE'RE GOING BACK TO THE RIVERFRONT.
JOCK BROGGLIN

AW, MAN!
WHAT'S WRONG?

BROGGLIN'S BOAT IS PULLING AWAY!
PUMPKINS CO.
HARBOR AUTHORITY
PUTPUTPUT

HEY!
PUT PUT PUT PUT PUT PUT

HEY, MISTER BROGGLIN!
WHAT?

WE NEED TO TALK TO YOU ABOUT YOUR TROLL BOOK!
YOU'RE THOSE KIDS WHO WERE PESTERING THE SHERIFF, AIN'TCHA?
PUTPUTPUTPUT
YOBBOS' REVENGE

"PESTERING" ISN'T EXACTLY A FAIR—
YEP, THAT'S US!

WELL, COME ON DOWN, THEN.

HERE, PULL ME IN ALONGSIDE.
YOBBOS' REVENGE

I HEARD Y'SAY **SOMETHING** ABOUT **INVISIBLE MONSTERS** TO OLD OBIE KRAUT, BUT I FIGURED YOU WERE JUST BEIN' **PUNKS.**
YOU KIDS **KNOW** ABOUT THE **TROLLS?**

YESSIR. ONE OF THEM **BIT** ME RIGHT IN THE **HELMET!**
HOLD ON THERE!

WHAT'S THAT IVORY-COLORED THING STICKING OUT OF THAT THERE **DENT?**

THIS? IT'S A TROLL TUSK.
BROKE OFF WHEN IT TRIED TO BITE ME. I WEDGED IT BACK INTO THE HELMET. AUTHENTIC BATTLE DAMAGE!
WAIT A MINUTE...
YOU CAN SEE IT?

WELL OF COURSE I CAN SEE IT!

!

HANG ON...
ARE YOU SAYING YOU CAN'T?!

NOPE. IT'S INVISIBLE, JUST LIKE THE TROLL THAT ATTACKED US.
HALIBUT ON A HANDLINE!
THAT'S WHAT I GET FOR THINKING A BUNCH OF DUMB KIDS KNOW ABOUT TROLLS.

TOSS THAT THING IN THE RIVER, AND THE HELMET WITH IT.
MAKING A TROPHY OF TROLL PARTS AIN'T RESPECTFUL TO THOSE FOLKS GOT THEMSELVES EATEN BY THE STINKERS, AND IT'S PROBABLY BAD LUCK, TOO.

NOW THROW ME BACK MY DOCK LINE!
NO WAY! IF YOU CAN SEE THE TROLLS, YOU CAN HELP US!

HELP, NOTHING! I'M UP AGAINST THE CLOCK HERE.

I'M NOT GOING TO WASTE MY TIME WITH A BUNCH OF GRADE SCHOOL KNUCKLEHEADS WHO DON'T EVEN KNOW THE GOAT TRICK!
!
GOATS!

WHAT ABOUT GOATS?
"NANNY HORN'D." NANNY IS AN OLD-TIMEY WORD FOR A FEMALE GOAT.
GOAT'S MILK!
WHERE ARE WE SUPPOSED TO GET GOAT'S MILK?
AND DO WE SPLASH IT ON THE LANTERN, OR PUT IT INSIDE?
LANTERN? WHAT ARE YOU NUMBSKULLS TALKING ABOUT?

DON'T YOU KNOW THE RHYME?
WHAT RHYME?
"THY LAMPS AWASH'D IN MILK OF NANNY HORN'D."

I DON'T KNOW ABOUT **LAMPS,** BUT YOU'RE SUPPOSED TO SPLASH GOAT'S MILK IN YOUR **EYES** IF YOU WANT TO **SEE TROLLS.**

EYES?
HUH.

I GUESS "LAMPS" IS, LIKE, POETIC.
HEY, UTILITY BELT! I TOLD YOU TO THROW THAT THING IN THE WATER.
JUST SAYING MY GOOD-BYES. THIS WAS MY SIXTH-FAVORITE GREEN HELMET.

AW, KEEP IT, I DON'T CARE. AND YOU'D BETTER GET OUT OF TOWN SOON.
YOU'VE GOT TWO, MAYBE THREE WEEKS BEFORE THE TROLLS START TO FEED.

WHAT DO YOU MEAN? A TROLL ATE SOME OF OUR CLASS-MATES **THIS MORNING.**

A TROLL **ATE** A **HUMAN?**
ARE YOU **SURE?**

WELL, WE DIDN'T SEE IT **HAPPEN,** BUT IT SEEMS **LIKELY.**
ONE OF THEM SURE TRIED TO EAT **ME!** THAT'S HOW ITS TUSK BROKE OFF IN MY HELMET.

NO NO NO
NO!

IT'S TOO SOON, TOO SOON!
WHAT'S TOO SOON?

THE TROLL FEAST! BOY OH BOY, YOUR FRIENDS MUST'VE **REALLY** PUT ONE ON THE SPOT FOR IT TO JUMP THE SCHEDULE BY SUCH A MARGIN.
I GOTTA GET MOVING. I'VE GOT SO MUCH LEFT TO DO, AND SO LITTLE—
...

THERE!
THERE, TEARING DOWN THE HILL!
YOBBOS' R

DANG IT, THAT'S RIGHT, YOU CAN'T SEE 'EM!

VRMMM
IT'S A TROLL!
QUICK, JUMP ON!

ROSARIO!

I DON'T HAVE A LIFE JACKET!
PUTPUTPUTP

JUST **JUMP,** ROSARIO! THERE'S AN INVISIBLE TROLL **HEADING RIGHT FOR YOU!**
I PROMISED MY DAD I'D NEVER GET ON A BOAT WITHOUT A LIFE JACKET!
HERE'S ONE!

CATCH, ROSARIO!
YOU'VE **GOT** TO WAIT FOR ROSARIO, MISTER BROGGLIN!
GET YOUR HAND OFF THAT THROTTLE!

CHUK
GOT IT!

YOBBOS' REVENGE

YOU DADGUM KIDS ALMOST GOT US **GRABBED!**
YOU ALMOST LEFT ROSARIO BEHIND!
HEY, AT LEAST WE GOT AWAY BEFORE THE TROLL GOT—
YOBBOS' REVENGE

CRASH!

DID WE HIT SOMETHING?
WE'RE STILL MOVING!

VROOMM
WE DIDN'T HIT ANYTHING, SOMETHING HIT US!
THE TROLL'S HANGING OFF THE STERN!
OKAY, PONYTAIL, YOU WANTED TO TAKE THE THROTTLE. NOW YOU CAN TAKE THE WHEEL!
KEEP US FROM VEERING STARBOARD!
WHICH WAY IS STARBOARD?
DON'T YOU KIDS KNOW ANYTHING?
THIS SIDE OF THE BOAT!
HEY, UTILITY BELT...
...HEADS UP!

THUNK

WHY ARE YOU THROWING HATCHETS AT CHILDREN?!

USE IT TO SMASH OPEN THOSE CRATES!
THERE ARE WEAPONS INSIDE THAT CAN STOP THE TROLL!

QUICK! IT'S CLIMBING ALONG THE SIDE, HEADING RIGHT FOR YOU!

SMASH

CANS OF PICKLED HERRING?

NO, **UNDER** THE HERRING! THE CRATES HAVE **FALSE BOTTOMS!**

SMASH
THE SHERIFF WAS RIGHT! HE **IS** A SMUGGLER!
PRETTY NEAT, HUH?
WHAT? **NO!**

IS THIS...

IS THIS **DEODORANT?**

IT'S RIGHT ON TOP OF YOU, KID!
SPRAY THAT DEODORANT!

SPRAY!

POP
POP

FSSHHSSH

ROARR
YEE-HAW! THAT GOT HIM!
SPLOOSH

YOU KIDS AIN'T SO BAD AFTER...

PONYTAIL, WHAT ARE YOU DOING?!

TURN THE WHEEL!
TURN THE WHEEL!
I'M TURNING IT AS HARD AS I CAN!

NO, NO! THE OTHER

WAAAAAAY
PUMPKINS CO.

BROGGLIN'S HIDING **SOMETHING** ON THAT BOAT. I CAN FEEL IT.
MAYBE, BUT—
SHERIFF'S DEPT

SHERI DEPT.

FIN

I'M **REALLY** SORRY ABOUT YOUR BOAT, MR. BROGGLIN.
BOAT, SHMOAT! I GOT NO AFFECTION FOR THAT TUB.
BUT I **DO** CARE ABOUT TAKING OUT THE COUNTY'S **TROLLS** BEFORE THEY GO AND **EAT** A BUNCH OF PEOPLE.
O'SHEA'S

BUT I CAN'T DO **THAT** RIGHT NOW BECAUSE **YOU** KNUCKLEHEADS HAVE GOTTEN ME **ARRESTED** ON SUSPICION OF **SMUGGLING!**
LET'S JUST CALL IT **SMUGGLING,** JOCK.
YOU'VE GOT, WHAT, A THOUSAND CANS OF O'SHEA'S DEODORANT STASHED? **TWO** THOUSAND?
O'SHEA'S
O'SHEA'S
O'SHE

IT'S **ILLEGAL** TO SELL AEROSOL HYGIENE PRODUCTS IN PUMPKINS COUNTY.
IT **IS? WHY?**
IT'S ONE OF THOSE OLD-TIMEY LAWS THAT NEVER GOT REPEALED. AEROSOLS USED TO HAVE OZONE-DEPLETING CHEMICALS IN THEM.

REALLY BAD FOR THE ENVIRONMENT.
WELL, **I** WASN'T **SELLING** THEM.

WELL, WE'VE GOT YOU ON **INTENT** TO SELL, THEN.
I DIDN'T "INTEND" TO **SELL** A **SINGLE CAN!** EVERY ONE OF THESE IS FOR **MY USE!**
HEY, SHERIFF, GET A LOAD OF **THIS** CONTRAPTION!

I **THINK** IT'S SOME KIND OF HIGH-TECH **SALES RACK.**
HIS BACK-ALLEY DEODORANT OPERATION IS FANCIER THAN WE THOUGHT!

THAT'S NOT A **SALES RACK,** YOU CHOWDER-HEADS, IT'S A...

-SIGH-
FINE. YOU GOT ME. IT'S A "SALES RACK."

JUST **BOOK ME,** SO I CAN GET MY COURT SUMMONS AND BE ON MY WAY.
AND **DON'T** LUMP THESE KNUCKLEHEAD **KIDS** IN WITH ME, NEITHER.
NICE **TRY,** BROGGLIN!

THESE CREEPS ARE A **CONSTANT** IRRITATION TO THE CITIZENS OF PUMPKINS COUNTY.

NOW THEY'VE BEEN CAUGHT HELPING **YOU** WITH YOUR **MUSK-RUNNING** OUTFIT—
FINN, WE'VE GOT A **LOT** OF EVIDENCE **AND** A SUSPECT TO BRING DOWN TO THE STATION...
O'SHEA'S

...AND WE'VE ONLY GOT **ONE** VEHICLE NOW.

...

FINE. FINE, WE CAUGHT OUR SMUGGLER.
THAT'S ENOUGH.

BUT OUR **JOB** IS TO **PROTECT** AND **SERVE** THIS COMMUNITY, AND WE'RE DOING **NEITHER** BY LETTING **THESE** TROUBLEMAKERS RUN **WILD.**
PSST!

LISTEN UP, YOU GOOBERS!
YOU'VE ONLY GOT A **FEW HOURS** BEFORE THE TROLLS **EAT** HALF THE PEOPLE IN THIS TOWN, SO GET YOURSELVES **VERY FAR AWAY.**

THE **CYCLE** HAS **BEGUN!**
ALL RIGHT, CRAZY PANTS, TIME TO GO.
AND KIDS?

I'VE SEEN YOU THREE TIMES TOO MANY TODAY.
SCRAM.
YOBBOS' OVEN

JEEZ!

DO YOU REALLY THINK THAT THE TROLLS ARE GOING TO EAT HALF THE TOWN?
WHAT DO YOU THINK HE MEANT BY "THE CYCLE"?
WHAT'S OUR PLAN TO STOP THEM? DO WE HAVE A PLAN?
ARE WE GOING TO BUST MR. BROGGLIN OUT OF JAIL?
I'VE BEEN MEANING TO MAKE A JAILBREAK KIT, BUT I HAVEN'T BEEN ABLE TO FIND A RACCOON OR A SUSAN B. ANTHONY COSTUME THAT WOULD STAND UP TO SCRUTINY.
HEY, SHOULD WE—
JARVIS!
WE'RE GOING TO GET GOAT'S MILK.
YOU KNOW WHERE WE CAN GET GOAT'S MILK?
VENABLE'S PIZZA
YEAH...
...I THINK I DO.
UNGHH. IT SMELLS WORSE OUT THERE THAN IT DID BY THE RIVER.
VENABLE'S! HOME OF THE FAMOUS TRIPLE GOAT CHEESE PIZZA.
AND I'M TELLING YOU THAT THERE'S NO TEN-FOR-TEN SPECIAL!
THEN WHY'D YOU POST IT ON YOUR TATTLER PAGE?
WE DO NOT USE BABY KANGAROO MEAT ON OUR VEGETARIAN PIZZAS! IF YOU DON'T DELETE THAT, WE'LL SUE!

THE ONLY GOAT CHEESE LEFT IN THE PLACE IS ON **THIS** SLICE OF DOUBLE GARLIC RED PEPPERSPLOSION WASABI BUFFALO **CHILI FANTASMO.**

WHAAA
AEIIEE
I'M BLIND! **BLIND!**
CAROL, THIS WAS A **TERRIBLE** IDEA!
IT WAS
AAA
THE BEST I COULD COME UP WITH, OKAAA

AUGGH
VENABLE'S
VENABLE'S PIZZA

WAAGHH
VENABLE'S
VENABLE'S PIZZA

UNGH
COUGH COUGH
RRR!
WOOF!
VENABLE'S
VENABLE'S PIZZA

OKAY. RUBBING PIZZA IN OUR EYES **WAS** A BAD IDEA.
BUT WE CAN SEE **TROLLS** NOW, RIGHT?
I DON'T KNOW. **I** DON'T SEE ANY.

AT LEAST ALL THOSE CRAZY SPICES KEPT US FROM SMELLING THIS ALLEY.
TEMPORARILY, AT LEAST.
YOU'RE RIGHT, IT **IS** WORSE HERE THAN IT WAS AT THE RIVERFRONT.
...
WHAT DO YOU THINK IS CAUSING IT? THOSE GREASE-TRAPS, OR THE DUMPSTERS?

I DON'T THINK WHAT **WE'RE** SMELLING IS **EITHER** OF THOSE THINGS.

YEEAAHH...
I THINK THE GOAT CHEESE **WORKED.**
HEY, CAN YOU SEE ME?
UM...
NO.

WAIT...**YOU'RE** THE KIDS FROM THE **RIVERFRONT!**
NO, WE'RE NOT!

OH, YES, YOU ARE! THAT'S **MY TUSK** STUCK IN **YOUR HEAD!**

YEAH...**YOU'RE** THE ONE WHO SPRAYED ME WITH **POISON** ON THAT BOAT!

I SHOULD **REALLY** BE FOCUSING ON WORK RIGHT NOW...
WE **ARE** UP AGAINST A TIGHT DEADLINE...

...BUT IT **IS YOUR FAULT** THAT WE'RE UNDER THE GUN HERE. YOU AND THOSE **OTHER** POISON-SPRAYING, **DELICIOUS** LITTLE **MONSTERS.**

"DELICIOUS"?!
SO ERNEST AND MARY **WERE** EATEN!

IF YOU'RE SPEAKING OF THE BIG GREEN-HIDE AND THE LITTLE BLUE-HIDE, THEN YES, **I ATE THEM!** IT WAS **REFLEX, SELF-DEFENSE.** I WAS UNDER **ATTACK!** AND NOW **I'M** ON THE HOOK FOR DISOBEYING **ORDERS.**
AND SINCE I'M **ALREADY IN** SO MUCH **TROUBLE...**

...I MIGHT AS WELL **TREAT** MYSELF TO AN **UNAUTHORIZED SNACK BREAK!**

ROAR!
CRUNCH

ROARR!
WATCH IT, KIDS!

ROAR!
IT'S GAINING ON US!

WHOA, HOLD UP!

BUSY ROAD!

GRAB HANDS!

HOLD ON TIGHT!

ROAR!
WHOA!
OOF!

?

SLAM

SCREEEEEEEEEEE

OHMYGOSHOHMYGOSH
ARE YOU GUYS OKAY?

HEEEEEY, BROTHER!
DON'T "HEY, BROTHER" ME! WHAT ARE YOU **DOING,** RIDING YOUR BIKES ACROSS TRAFFIC LIKE THAT?!
WE WEREN'T!

YOU DIDN'T HIT **US,** YOU HIT A **TROLL.**
OUR BIKES WERE JUST STUCK IN THE SPIKES ON ITS BACK.
OOH, JARVIS, DON'T LET ME FORGET TO SPECULATE ON THE FUNCTIONAL PURPOSE OF THE TROLLS' **DORSAL SPINES** WHEN WE MAKE THE ENTRY IN OUR CREATURE COMPENDIUM.
BACK SPIKES. GOT IT.
TROLLS AGAIN?!

GUYS, I'VE GOT **WAY** MORE IMPORTANT THINGS TO DEAL WITH RIGHT NOW THAN **YOUR** TROLL ISSUES.
MOM'S GOING TO PULL MY DRIVING PRIVILEGES FOR **SURE** WHEN SHE SEES THIS DENT, **AND CLARA BROKE UP WITH ME!**
SHE DID? GERARD, I'M SO SORRY. DID SHE SAY WHY?
NO!
SHE DIDN'T EVEN **CALL** ME. SHE SENT A NOTE TO ME OVER **TATTLER!**
IT'S BEEN A BAD DAY FOR **EVERYBODY** ON TATTLER.
I DON'T BELIEVE IT! YOU AND CLARA ARE MEANT TO BE, MAN!
UM, GUYS, THE TROLL IS STARTING TO MOVE.
UNGH
GERARD, WE **REALLY** NEED A RIDE. LIKE, **RIGHT NOW.**
NO WAY!
I'VE GOT TO FIND CLARA AND FIND OUT WHAT'S GOING ON.
CAN'T YOU JUST **CALL** HER, BIG BROTHER?
MY PHONE'S NOT WORKING. I CAN'T GET A SIGNAL.
HEY!
PLEASE, GERARD! IT'S A MATTER OF LIFE AND DEATH!
-SIGH-
FINE, GET IN.
THANKS!
HEY, HOLD
UUUNGH
WHOA! PRETTY DIZZY.

GO, GERARD, GO GO GO!
CLICK!
ARE YOU GUYS ALL BUCKLED?

AAGH! NO TIME, NO TIME!
THUD!

WE'RE NOT MOVING UNTIL YOU'RE ALL WEARING SEAT BELTS.
DOES SOMEONE NEED TO COME AROUND TO THE FRONT SEAT?
NO!

OH, MAN. GIMME A SECOND.

-MMPH!-

BLARFF

OH. OH, MAN. I THINK I HAVE A **CONCUSSION.**
WE'RE BUCKLED, GERARD! **GO!**

HEY, WAIT, I'M NOT DONE EATING YOU!
VROOM!

...THIS WHOLE TROLL THING **MIGHT** BE A BIGGER PROBLEM THAN WE **THOUGHT.**

GUYS, I THINK WE CAN LET UP WITH THE COVERT INFILTRATION STUFF. SHERIFF OBIE AND DEPUTY FINN **AREN'T HERE.**

THIS NOTE SAYS THAT THERE ARE DISTURBANCES ALL OVER TOWN. THEY WANT PEOPLE TO JUST WAIT HERE IF THEY HAVE AN EMERGENCY.

WE'RE THE KIDS THAT CRASHED YOUR BOAT.

WE'RE IN DISGUISE.

YEAH, I WAS COMPLETELY FOOLED.
WHERE'S THE SHERIFF? IS HE GOING TO LET ME OUT OF HERE, OR WHAT?

HE AND DEPUTY FINN LEFT. THEY HAD TO RESPOND TO SOME CALLS.
SO WE'RE BUSTIN' YOU OUT!

WELL, GREAT, GET MOVING! WE HAVEN'T GOT MUCH TIME.
I'LL GO FIND THE KEY TO THE CELL!

WHILE HE'S DOING THAT, CAN YOU FILL US IN ON WHAT'S HAPPENING?
WHERE DID ALL THESE TROLLS COME FROM?
HOW COME YOU KNOW HOW TO SEE THEM?
WHAT DID YOU MEAN WHEN YOU SAID "THE CYCLE HAS BEGUN"?

-SIGH-
I SUPPOSE I OUGHT TO START AT THE BEGINNING.

WHEN I WAS A KID, NEARABOUTS YOUR AGE, OUR CLASS HAD A FIELD TRIP TO A LOCAL FARM.

I WAS MAKING SOME TROUBLE FOR ONE OF MY CLASSMATES, THIS KID RANDALL WHO THOUGHT HE WAS REALLY FUNNY.

THINGS GOT OUT OF HAND.

LONG STORY SHORT, A COUPLE OF OTHER KIDS STEPPED IN TO HELP RANDALL, AND IN THE STRUGGLE WE KNOCKED OVER A BIG CAN OF **GOAT'S MILK.**
HEY!

I FOUND A BOX WITH A LABEL ON IT THAT SAYS "SPARE HOLDING-CELL KEY."

IT'S LOCKED.

I'LL KEEP LOOKING.

THERE WERE FIVE OF US THAT GOT GOAT'S MILK IN OUR EYES THAT DAY.

WE THOUGHT WE HAD NOTHING IN COMMON. DIDN'T EVEN **LIKE** EACH OTHER.

BUT ON THE BUS RIDE BACK TO SCHOOL, WE REALIZED THAT WE **DID** HAVE SOMETHING IN COMMON, AFTER ALL:

WE COULD SEE THE **TROLLS.**

WAIT, THE TROLLS WERE AROUND **WAY BACK THEN?**
PONYTAIL, THE TROLLS THAT LIVE **HERE** HAVE BEEN AROUND FOR **GENERATIONS!**

THEY CAME HERE HIDDEN AMONGST A GROUP OF **NORWEGIAN IMMIGRANTS,** LANDING IN WHAT WOULD EVENTUALLY BECOME **PUMPKINS COUNTY.**
IT WAS AN IDEAL DESTINATION FOR THE TROLLS. FRONTIER LIFE WAS **STRESSFUL.**

TROLLS **LIKE** BEING **STRESSED?**
OF **COURSE** NOT, SWEATERSET. BUT THEY **DO** WANT THEIR **FOOD** TO BE STRESSED.

TROLLS **NEED** THE HUMANS THAT THEY INTEND TO EAT TO SIMMER IN THEIR OWN STRESS HORMONES FOR WEEKS, EVEN MONTHS, BEFORE THEY'RE DEVOURED.
IF HUMANS STRESS LONG ENOUGH, THEIR BODIES PRODUCE **CHEMICALS** THAT HAVE AN EFFECT ON THE TROLLS' **DIGESTIVE SYSTEMS.**

TROLL CLANS **HIBERNATE** TOGETHER FOR DECADES AT A TIME.
Z
Z
Z
Z
THE **STRESS CHEMICALS** ARE WHAT LET THEM **LINK UP** AND **SLEEP** AS A **SINGLE UNIT.**

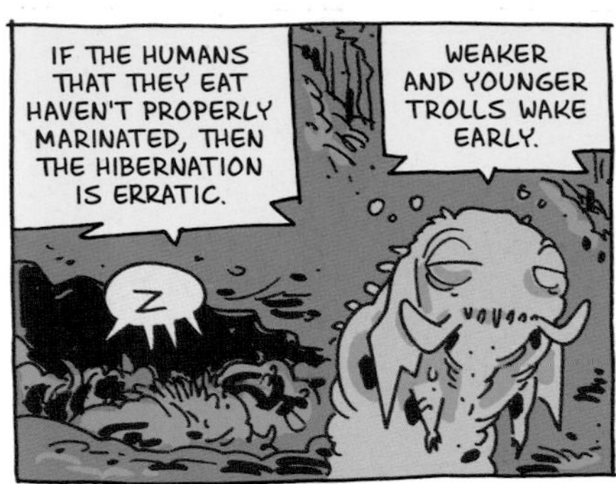
IF THE HUMANS THAT THEY EAT HAVEN'T PROPERLY MARINATED, THEN THE HIBERNATION IS ERRATIC.
WEAKER AND YOUNGER TROLLS WAKE EARLY.
Z

WITHOUT SUFFICIENT REST, THEY LOSE THEIR INVISIBILITY, AND WITH NO CLAN TO PROTECT THEM THEY USUALLY END UP GETTING TAKEN OUT BY WHATEVER HEROES LIVE NEARBY.

SO TROLLS SEEK OUT PEOPLE UNDER STRESS.
TROLLS **MAKE** THE STRESS, WHITEWASH!

EVER HEAR OF THE **BLACK PLAGUE?** THE **IRISH POTATO FAMINE?** THE **DUST BOWL?** THE **GREAT DEPRESSION?**

TROLL PLOTS! EVERY ONE OF THEM A GRAND UNDERTAKING WHOSE SOLE PURPOSE WAS TO CAUSE PEOPLE PERPETUAL **WORRY.**

OH, YEAH. THAT'S THE STUFF YOUR BOOK WAS TALKING ABOUT.
THE EVIDENCE IS ALL AROUND, WHITEWASH, BUT IT DOESN'T BECOME **CLEAR** UNLESS SOMEONE SHINES A LIGHT ON IT FOR YOU. US? **WE** WERE TOLD OF THE TROLL PLOTS BY A LOCAL FISHERMAN:

OLD MAN LUTEFISK, LAST OF THE GREAT **TROLLFIGHTERS.**

LUTEFISK TOLD US TO SCRAM. BUT WHEN WE FOUND OUT THAT THE TROLLS INTENDED TO EAT THE TOWNSPEOPLE...INCLUDING OUR FAMILIES...WE DECIDED TO FIGHT BACK.

THE OLD MAN AGREED TO TRAIN US. HE'D CALCULATED THAT WE HAD ONLY THREE DAYS UNTIL THE TROLLS' FEAST, AND WE NEEDED EVERY MINUTE OF IT.

THEIR FEAST?
YEAH, THEIR FEAST. IT'S WHAT ALL THEIR PLANS ARE LEADING TO!

HUMAN STRESS CHEMICALS DON'T JUST **KEEP** THE TROLLS HIBERNATING...

...THEY'RE WHAT STARTS THE HIBERNATION PROCESS IN THE FIRST PLACE!

AS SOON AS A TROLL EATS A HUMAN, THE PROCESS BEGINS, AND WITHIN A **FEW HOURS** ITS **WHOLE CLAN** WILL FALL INTO YEARS-LONG SLUMBER!

THEY WANT TO EAT AS MUCH AS POSSIBLE IN A VERY SHORT WINDOW OF TIME, SO WHEN THEY RECKON THE HUMANS ARE **RIPE** THEY'LL LURE THEM ALL TO SOME **SECRET SPOT...**
...SOMEWHERE THAT **STINKS,** SO THAT THEIR SMELL DOESN'T BETRAY THEIR PRESENCE, DESPITE THEIR INVISIBILITY...

...AND THEY **FEAST!**
HEY!

I DIDN'T FIND THE KEY TO THE BOX.

BUT I **DID** FIND MY CONFISCATED **LOCK PICK SET!**

I'M GONNA GET TO WORK.

WE THREW EVERYTHING WE HAD INTO STOPPING THE APPROACHING FEAST.
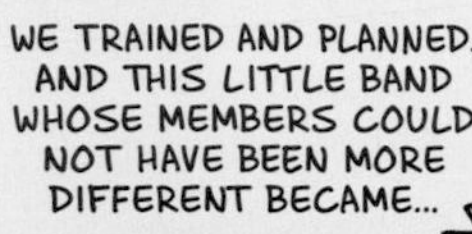
WE TRAINED AND PLANNED. AND THIS LITTLE BAND WHOSE MEMBERS COULD NOT HAVE BEEN MORE DIFFERENT BECAME...

...FRIENDS.

MORE THAN FRIENDS, EVEN. BROTHERS AND SISTERS IN ARMS.

WE CALLED OURSELVES **THE YOBBOS.**
AND WE HAD ONE MISSION...

...TO PUT AN **END** TO THE TROLLS OF PUMPKINS COUNTY, **ONCE AND FOR ALL.**

WE FAILED.

DO YOU HAVE ANY IDEA HOW NAIVE WE WERE, THINKING THAT A GROUP OF KIDS COULD TAKE ON A BUNCH OF MONSTERS?
IT WAS A **MASSACRE.**

RICKY WAS TORN TO PIECES THE MINUTE WE WALKED INTO THEIR LAIR.

TABITHA WAS NOTHING BUT A SMEAR ON THE FLOOR OF THE CAVE AFTER A TROLL DROVE HIS FIST DOWN ON HER.

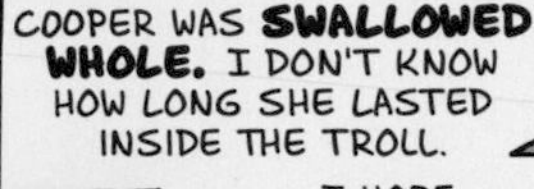
COOPER WAS **SWALLOWED WHOLE.** I DON'T KNOW HOW LONG SHE LASTED INSIDE THE TROLL.

I HOPE HER STRUGGLE WAS A SHORT ONE.

ONE OF THE TROLLS STARTED TO EAT **ME.** MY LEGS WERE GONE WITH ITS FIRST BITE.

FUNNY RANDALL, WHO IN A FEW SHORT DAYS HAD BECOME THE VERY BEST FRIEND I'VE EVER HAD, CAME TO MY RESCUE.

HE LAUNCHED HIMSELF AT THE TROLL, LIKE A GREAT WARRIOR IN SOME ANCIENT MYTH.

BUT RANDALL **WASN'T** A GREAT WARRIOR. HE WAS JUST A BRAVE KID WITH A HEART TOO BIG TO REALIZE THAT A JERK LIKE **ME** WASN'T WORTH SAVING.

WE COULD'T STOP THEM. THE TROLLS WENT ON TO FEAST AS PLANNED.

MY **PARENTS** WERE AMONG THE ONES DEVOURED TO FUEL THE TROLLS' LONG RESPITE.

LUTEFISK TOOK ME IN, AND **TRAINED** ME IN THE DYING ART OF **TROLLFIGHTING.**

THE OLD MAN FIGURED I'D HAVE TO FACE THEM EVENTUALLY. ONE **DID** EAT MY LEGS, AFTER ALL.

ONCE A TROLL HAS SUPPED ON YOUR FLESH, IT'S **BOUND TO YOU FOREVER,** AND WILL ALWAYS SNIFF YOU OUT AND **FIND** YOU AFTER IT AWAKENS FROM ITS HIBERNATION.

TROLLFIGHTERS **NEVER** DIE OF OLD AGE. IF THEY'RE NOT KILLED IN COMBAT, THEN THEY'RE EVENTUALLY SNIFFED OUT BY A TROLL THAT'S EATEN SOME PART OF THEM.

BEST A TROLLFIGHTER CAN HOPE FOR IS TO TAKE ONE WITH HIM WHEN HE GOES.

THE OLD MAN BOUGHT IT IN RIO DE JANEIRO. HAD HIS HEAD BITTEN OFF BY A PARTICULARLY NASTY ÖSTFOLD BLUE TUSKER THAT HAD TAKEN HIS PINKY FINGER WHEN HE WAS A YOUNG MAN.
HEY!

I JUST REALIZED THAT I'M ONLY PICKING **THIS** LOCK SO THAT I CAN OPEN **THAT** ONE.

IT MAKES MORE SENSE TO JUST **FORGET** ABOUT THIS SPARE KEY BOX AND **INSTEAD** PICK THE LOCK OF THE HOLDING-CELL **DOOR.**

I'LL GET RIGHT ON IT!

FOR YEARS I'VE WAITED FOR THE PUMPKINS COUNTY TROLL CLAN TO AWAKEN SO THAT I CAN STOP THEM ONCE AND FOR ALL.

BUT I DON'T KNOW WHERE THEIR NEW LAIR IS BECAUSE I DON'T KNOW WHAT THEIR PLOT IS FOR RAISING EVERYONE'S STRESS LEVELS!

EVERYONE SEEMS STRESSED, ALL RIGHT, BUT IF THEY'RE SHARING A COMMON CONCERN, **I** CAN'T FIGURE WHAT IT IS!
SOME PEOPLE ARE UPSET ABOUT WORK, SOME PEOPLE ARE UPSET ABOUT POLITICS, SOME PEOPLE ARE UPSET ABOUT TIIG FOLKS IN THEIR FAMILIES...
CLICK
GOT IT! YOU'RE FREE!

COME ON! WE'VE GOT TO GET TO THE EVIDENCE LOCKER!

THAT LOCKER HOLDS OUR ONLY HOPE OF VICTORY. SOMETHING WE CAN USE AGAINST THE TROLLS.

IT'S NO EASY TASK TO BEAT A TROLL IN A FIGHT, AND IT'S NEAR ON **IMPOSSIBLE** WHEN THERE'S MORE THAN ONE OF THEM AROUND.

YOU MIGHT BEAT ONE OR TWO IF THEY'RE ALONE, BUT THERE'S NO WAY TO TAKE OUT A **WHOLE CLAN.** AT LEAST, IT HASN'T EVER BEEN DONE BEFORE.

BUT I THINK I'VE FOUND A WAY.
DOES IT HAVE SOMETHING TO DO WITH A **TRILL?**

WHAT THE HECK IS A TRILL?
IT WAS IN A POEM ABOUT KILLING TROLLS. "IF SEEK YE MONSTERS' END AS END BETIDE, A TRILL FROM PASSION'S FOUNTAINHEAD DECLARE."

COME ON, KID, YOU'RE JUST SPOUTIN' GIBBERISH. THIS IS A **TROLL FIGHT,** NOT A **POETRY RECITATION.**
ALL RIGHT, UTILITY BELT, PUT THOSE LOCK-PICK TOOLS TO WORK.

IF YOUR FRIEND LUTEFISK TRAINED YOU AS A TROLLFIGHTER, SHOULDN'T HE HAVE TAUGHT YOU WHATEVER OLD VERSES MIGHT GIVE DIRECTIONS ON HOW TO STOP THEM?

THE **EARLIEST** TROLLFIGHTERS WERE MINSTRELS, BARDS. THEY SANG SONGS AND WROTE POETRY TO HELP VILLAGERS REMEMBER HOW TO DEAL WITH THE TROLL SCOURGE AFTER THEY'D LEFT. BUT **THEIR** KIND DIED OUT A **LONG TIME AGO**.
DURING THE MIDDLE AGES, A **NEW** KIND OF TROLLFIGHTER EMERGED.
WARRIORS!
HARDSCRABBLE MEN AND WOMEN WHO HAD NO TIME FOR THE NONSENSE OF THEIR SONG-HAPPY ANCESTORS.

THAT WOULD STILL MEAN TRYING TO TAKE OUT THE TROLLS **ONE BY ONE,** AND THEY'RE **TOO POWERFUL** FOR ANYONE TO DO **THAT.**

THE TROLLS WILL HERD THE VICTIMS TO THEIR LAIR, BUT I DON'T KNOW WHERE THEIR LAIR IS.

IF I COULD JUST FIGURE OUT WHAT THEIR PLOT IS, HOW THEY'RE MANAGING TO STRESS EVERYONE OUT, THAT MIGHT BE ENOUGH OF A CLUE, BUT I'M STUMPED.

THIS IS WHERE THE TROLL THAT ATE MY LEGS LIVES.

WHEN THE SHERIFF BROUGHT ME TO THE STATION EARLIER FOR QUESTIONING, IT STARTED SNIFFING ME OUT, AND IT ALMOST CAUGHT ME WHEN I PULLED BACK TO SHORE FOR YOU KNUCKLEHEADS.

THE ONE THAT ATE YOUR LEGS... YOU SAY IT HAS A SPOT AROUND ITS EYE?

WE'RE NOT LUCKY.

SLAM

SCRAPE
SCRATCH
BANG
WELL, DANG.
BANG
THUMP
SCRATCH
BANG

GUESS THIS IS THE END OF THE LINE.
HEY!
YOU'RE A **TROLLFIGHTER.** YOU CAN'T JUST **GIVE UP.**
I DIDN'T SAY I WAS GIVING UP. I'LL FIGHT, ALL RIGHT, BUT WE AIN'T WALKING OUT OF HERE ALIVE. TOO MANY TROLLS OUT THERE.

PART OF BEING A TROLLFIGHTER IS **ACCEPTING** YOUR DEATH WHEN IT FINDS YOU.
HEY, **WE'RE** NOT TROLLFIGHTERS. **WE** DON'T HAVE TO BE ALL ZEN ABOUT MAYBE DYING.
TOUGH COOKIES, PRINCESS.
BANG
SCRATCH

BEEP BEEP
DYING IS WHAT WE'RE ABOUT TO **DO.**
BOMB ARMED

WHAT ABOUT YOUR PLAN TO TAKE OUT THE TROLLS' LAIR?
CLICK

EVEN IF YOU TAKE OUT **THESE** TROLLS WITH YOUR DEODORANT BOMB, THE **OTHERS** WILL STILL BE AROUND TO FEAST ON THE PEOPLE OF PUMPKINS COUNTY!

CAN'T HAVE **EVERYTHING** YOU WANT IN LIFE, WHITEWASH.
ME?

I'M JUST GLAD I'LL BE TAKING OLD SPOT ALONG WITH ME.
SKRR
SCRCH
RIP
BAM
THUD
BAM

THAT'S IT, UGLIES. COME ON IN.
12 CANS DEODORANT

HEY!

IT'S YOU KIDS AGAIN!

I GOT HIT BY A **CAR** BECAUSE OF YOU LITTLE **MEATBALLS!**
YOU GOT HIT BY A CAR BECAUSE YOU WERE TRYING TO **EAT** US!
GET READY WHEN I SAY "ROLL!"

THAT'S THE **FOOD CHAIN,** MAN! **I'M** AT THE **TOP, YOU'RE** AT THE **BOTTOM.**
POP

I'M **GOING** TO EAT YOU. THE POLITE THING FOR **YOU** TO DO IS MAKE THAT TASK AS EASY FOR ME AS POSSIBLE.
SORRY, SPOT. THAT'S NOT HOW WE...

...ROLL!

!

ROAR
ACK!
-COUGH-

HOP ON, MITCHELL!

YOINK

HA!

YOU THINK YOU CAN OUTRUN **ALL** OF US?

YOU WON'T BE CHASING **THEM,** YOU PEOPLE-EATING SACK OF **STINK.**
THIS MIGHT BE THE **END** FOR OLD JOCK, BUT TAKING FIVE TROLLS WITH ME? THAT AIN'T SUCH A BAD WAY TO GO.

TIME TO **FRESHEN UP.**
CLICK

KABOOM

AAAAGH

SPLASH

GASP

WHERE'S JARVIS? WHERE'S ROSARIO?
I DON'T KNOW!

SPLLPK!

PLEASE BE OKAY.

HUH?
BLUB

FOOM

YES!
GASP GASP

ARE YOU GUYS OKAY? WHAT HAPPENED?
JARVIS'S PANT LEG WAS CAUGHT ON THE CHAIR. IT WAS PULLING HIM DOWN.
HE'S NOT BREATHING.

ROSARIO KEPT HIM FROM SINKING TO THE BOTTOM, BUT WE COULDN'T SWIM UP WITH THE CHAIR. IT WAS TOO HEAVY.
WE'VE GOT TO GET HIM TO SHORE!

WHAT WAS THAT UNDERWATER BLAST?
I SET OFF HIS **PANTS EJECTOR.**
ONCE JARVIS WAS FREE FROM THE WHEELCHAIR, WE COULD PULL HIM TO THE SURFACE.

HE'S STILL NOT BREATHING!

DOES HE HAVE A PULSE?
UM
NO
I DON'T FEEL ONE

OH MY GOSH
I'M GONNA DO CPR.

KEEP HIS HEAD TILTED BACK.
ONE
TWO
THREE
FOUR

FIVE
SIX

SEVEN

EIGHT
NINE

TE—
COUGH
EGHGHK
JARVIS!

COUGH
COUGH
THAT'S IT, BUDDY! GET IT ALL OUT!
JARVIS!

ARE YOU OKAY?
CAN YOU BREATHE?
SAY SOMETHING!

-COUGH-
-COUGH-
WHY DON'T I HAVE ANY PANTS?

STILL NO SIGNAL.
CAROL, I DON'T NEED AN AMBULANCE. MY CHEST IS A LITTLE SORE, BUT OTHERWISE I'M FINE.

BUT THERE'S A PHONE TOWER RIGHT DOWN THE STREET.
I SHOULD BE GETTING GREAT SERVICE HERE.
PEOPLE HAVE BEEN HAVING PHONE TROUBLE ALL DAY.

I'M NOT ABLE TO GET ONLINE, EITHER.
NO MESSAGING, NO E-MAIL, NOTHING.
THE ONLY THING THAT SEEMS TO BE WORKING IS TATTLER.
OH MY GOSH! HAVE YOU KIDS BEEN SWIMMING?
FANCY SPRING SP

NOT ON PURPOSE!
YOU NEED TO GET TO THE HOSPITAL RIGHT AWAY!
SERIOUSLY, I'M FINE! SORE CHEST, LITTLE BIT OF A COUGH, THAT'S IT.
THERE'S A KILLER BACTERIA IN THE COUNTY'S WATER SUPPLY. YOU COULD BE INFECTED!

GREAT. AS IF WE DIDN'T HAVE ENOUGH TO STRESS ABOUT ALREADY!
HOLD IT RIGHT THERE, YOU!

WHO, US?
YES, YOU!
WHAT PROOF DO YOU HAVE THAT YOU'RE NOT FROM GREENLAND?

UM...NONE, I GUESS.
IT'S NOT THE SORT OF THING I'VE EVER HAD TO PROVE BEFORE.
THAT'S EXACTLY THE SORT OF THING A GREENLANDER WOULD SAY!
BEAT 'EM DOWN, LADIES! IT'S OUR PATRIOTIC DUTY!

WHOA, THERE!
WHY DO YOU WANT TO FIGHT PEOPLE FROM GREENLAND?
BECAUSE THE GREENLANDERS HAVE INVADED!
THEY'VE ATTACKED THE CAPITOL AND ARE SENDING AN ARMY SWEEPING ACROSS THE COUNTRY.
THREE MONTHS!

ONLY THREE MONTHS UNTIL THE ASTEROID HITS!
ASTEROID?
WORTHLESS! IT'S ALL WORTHLESS! YEARS OF SAVING, FOR NOTHING!

WHAT IS GOING ON?!
PHONES ARE DOWN, THE INTERNET IS DOWN, THE INVADERS HAVE SHUT OFF ALL MEANS OF COMMUNICATION.
EXCEPT FOR TATTLER. IT'S WORKING.

YES, THANK HEAVENS FOR TATTLER! IT'S THE ONLY WAY THAT THE RESISTANCE CAN KEEP US INFORMED ABOUT THE INVASION!
WE'RE ALL SUPPOSED TO RENDEZVOUS AT THE CITY DUMP. STRENGTH IN NUMBERS, KIDS!

SEEMS LIKE A LOT HAS HAPPENED SINCE WE FLEW OUT OF THE SHERIFF'S STATION.
YEAH. IT "SEEMS" LIKE A LOT HAS HAPPENED.
SCREEEEEE!

AW, JEEZ! I THOUGHT YOU GUYS WERE AT THE DUMP!

HEY, BIG BROTHER!
WAIT, YOU MEAN THERE REALLY ARE INVADERS FROM GREENLAND?
WHAT?
NEVER MIND. FORGET WHATEVER WEIRD STUFF YOU'RE DOING.
MOM SENT ME A MESSAGE OVER TATTLER SAYING THAT YOU HAD AN ACCIDENT AT THE DUMP. I WAS HEADING THERE NOW!

WE HAVEN'T BEEN TO THE DUMP, AND I HAVEN'T TALKED TO MOM ALL DAY!
THIS DOESN'T MAKE ANY SENSE.
OH, YES IT DOES!
COME ON, GERARD. WE'RE GOING WITH YOU...

...TO THE CITY DUMP.

THOSE NESTS ARE EMPTY. ALL OF THE TROLLS HAVE MOVED ON TO THEIR LAIR NOW, I SUSPECT.
YOU THINK IT'S THE DUMP, DON'T YOU?
BROGGLIN DID SAY THE LAIR WOULD BE SOMEPLACE SMELLY SO THAT THE TROLLS COULD GO UNDISCOVERED.

I THINK THAT THE TROLLS ARE TRICKING PEOPLE INTO DELIVERING **THEMSELVES** TO THE BIG TROLL FEAST.

THE TATTLER MESSAGE TELLING GERARD TO GO TO THE DUMP WAS A LIE, AND IT PROBABLY WASN'T SENT BY MITCHELL'S MOM.

I DON'T THINK THAT GREENLAND WOULD INVADE OUR COUNTRY, SO THOSE OLD LADIES WERE PROBABLY TRICKED, TOO.

KILLER BACTERIA, FINANCIAL COLLAPSE, APOCALYPTIC ASTEROIDS...EVERYONE'S FREAKED OUT ABOUT DIFFERENT THINGS, AND EVERYONE SEEMS TO BE GETTING THEIR INFO THROUGH **TATTLER!**

I THINK THAT THE TROLLS HAVE GOTTEN CONTROL OF EVERYONE'S **TATTLER ACCOUNTS** AND ARE USING THEM TO STEER PEOPLE TOWARD THE DUMP.
THAT MUST BE WHY ALL OF THOSE TROLL NESTS WE'VE SEEN HAVE **COMPUTERS** IN THEM. THE TROLLS ARE **HACKING TATTLER!**
WAIT, YOU MEAN THAT THE MESSAGES COMING THROUGH TATTLER **AREN'T REAL?**

WOOOOOOO!

WHAT ARE—
CLARA DIDN'T BREAK UP WITH HIM, AFTER ALL.
MY WORLD, SO RECENTLY BEREFT OF HOPE AND HAPPINESS, IS BUILT ANEW WITH THESE GLAD TIDINGS, LITTLE BRO.
ARE THE TROLLS RESPONSIBLE FOR THE PHONES AND THE INTERNET NOT WORKING, TOO?
THAT'S PROBABLY A SAFE BET, SINCE TATTLER'S STILL ACCESSIBLE.

IF THEY TOOK DOWN ALL OTHER COMMUNICATION, THEY COULD MAKE IT IMPOSSIBLE FOR PEOPLE TO FIGURE OUT THAT THEY'RE BEING TRICKED INTO GOING TO THE DUMP.

YOU JUST SAID THAT PEOPLE ARE BEING TRICKED INTO COMING HERE.

IF SOMETHING **DANGEROUS** IS GOING ON, THEN I CAN'T JUST LET YOU CATS RUN RIGHT...

...

HOLD ON, CUPCAKE!
YOUR PARAMOUR WILL SOON BE AT YOUR SIDE!

BROGGLIN WASN'T LYING WHEN HE SAID THAT THE TROLLS WOULD EAT HALF THE TOWN.
THE ONLY TIME I'VE EVER SEEN THIS MANY PUMPKINS COUNTY FOLKS IN ONE PLACE IS AT THE HARVEST FESTIVAL.
WE'VE GOT TO DO **SOMETHING** TO STOP THE TROLLS.

I CAN'T **STAND** THE THOUGHT OF THEM EATING ALL OF THESE INNOCENT PEOPLE.
THEY'RE NOT **ALL** INNOCENT.
WELL, HEY, **CREEPS.**

WHAT DO YOU WANT, MADISON?
ARE YOU GUYS OKAY?

YEAH, WHY?

KELSEY STOUT POSTED AN EMERGENCY THING ON THE SCHOOL PAPER'S TATTLER PAGE.
SHE SAID THAT A BUNCH OF STUDENTS WERE IN A BAD ACCIDENT AT THE DUMP WORKING ON THEIR IMPROVE-THE-TOWN ASSIGNMENT.
I'M HERE TO HELP, IF I CAN.
I WOULDN'T TRUST ANYTHING YOU READ ON TATTLER RIGHT NOW.

YOU GUYS ARE REAL JERKS, YOU KNOW THAT?
YOU COULD AT LEAST **PRETEND** TO CARE ABOUT YOUR CLASSMATES.
WE CARE PLENTY! IT'S JUST THAT TATTLER HAS BEEN TAKEN OVER BY **TROLLS.**

THE ONLY PERSON I CAN THINK OF WHO'S BROKEN INTO SOMEONE ELSE'S TATTLER ACCOUNT IS **YOU,** CAROL PONDICHERRY.
AND I'LL GET THAT VIDEO BACK ONLINE, TOO, JUST YOU WAIT.

GREAT. NOW **I'M** MARINATING IN STRESS HORMONES.

FOR A FEW MINUTES I ACTUALLY FORGOT ABOUT HOW MANY PEOPLE WATCHED THAT VIDEO OF ME SINGING.
DON'T WORRY, ROSARIO. PEOPLE FORGET THAT STUFF PRETTY QUICK.
LOOK, MAUDE, IT'S THAT GIRL WHO WAS SINGING THAT SONG!

HEY, YOUR VIDEO WAS **AWESOME.**
QUIT DAWDLING, BEAUMONT! IF WE AREN'T IN LINE SOON, THE BANK'LL TAKE THE HOUSE!

COME ON!
BASKERVILLE : PUMPKINS COUNTY
-SIGH-

DO WE HAVE A PLAN?
YEAH...

...WE **STOP THE TROLLS.**
THAT'S NOT A **PLAN,** THAT'S A **GOAL.**

OH.
THEN NO, NO PLAN.
TAKE A LOOK OVER THERE, GUYS.

THE TROLLS SEEM TO BE CLUSTERED AROUND THAT BIG **TOWER.**

WELL...
I GUESS THAT'S WHERE WE'RE HEADING.

THEY'RE LOOKING RIGHT AT US.
THEY'RE LOOKING RIGHT AT **EVERYONE.** JUST ACT LIKE YOU CAN'T SEE THEM.

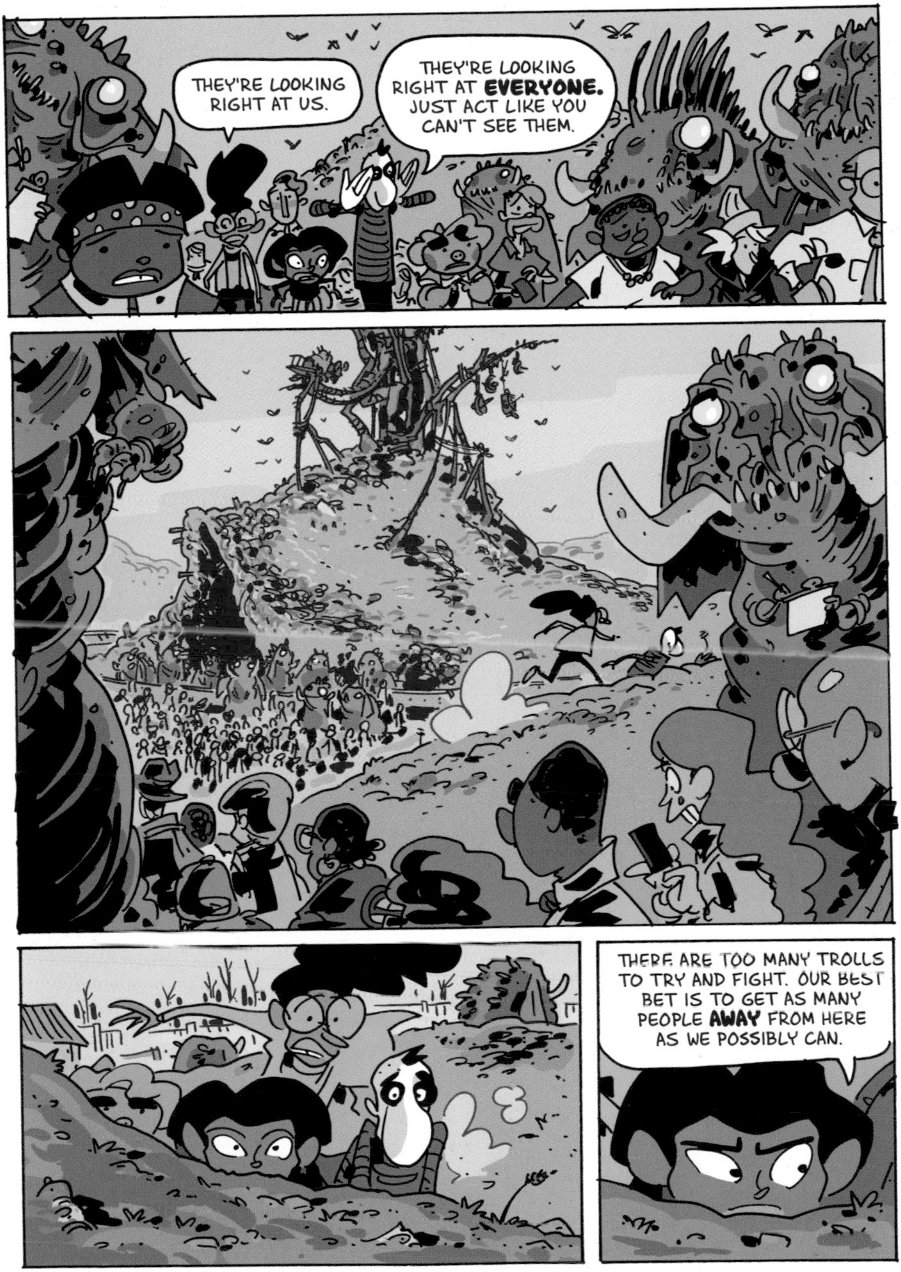

THERE ARE TOO MANY TROLLS TO TRY AND FIGHT. OUR BEST BET IS TO GET AS MANY PEOPLE **AWAY** FROM HERE AS WE POSSIBLY CAN.

IF WE TRY TO WARN ANYONE, THE TROLLS MIGHT JUST START **DEVOURING** EVERYONE.
AND SINCE NO ONE ELSE CAN **SEE** THE TROLLS, NOBODY WOULD LISTEN TO US, ANYWAY.

THAT TOWER HAS ANTENNAS AND DISHES AND STUFF ALL OVER IT. DOLLARS TO DONUTS IT'S WHAT THEY'RE USING TO CONTROL OUR COMMUNICATIONS.
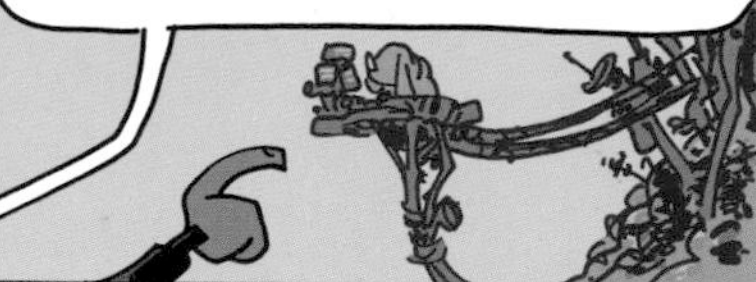

CAROL, IF WE CAN GET YOU UP TO THE CONTROL PLATFORM, COULD YOU HACK INTO THEIR SIGNAL?
WE COULD SEND A MESSAGE OUT TO KEEP ANYONE ELSE FROM COMING, AND MAYBE WARN THE PEOPLE ALREADY HERE.

I COULD TRY. IT DEPENDS ON WHAT SYSTEM THEY'RE USING.
FOLLOW ME, AND STICK CLOSE.

EWW!

YOU'D THINK BY NOW I WOULD BE **USED** TO CLIMBING THROUGH GROSS STUFF TO FIGHT MONSTERS, BUT NOPE. STILL NOT USED TO IT.

TAP
TAP
TAP

TAP TIP

TAP TAP TAP

HEY, WHY ARE YOU CLIMBING UP HERE?
THERE'S ONLY SUPPOSED TO BE **ONE** TROLL IN THE TOWER!
-OOF!-
YEAH, WELL...
...I'M TAKING OVER.

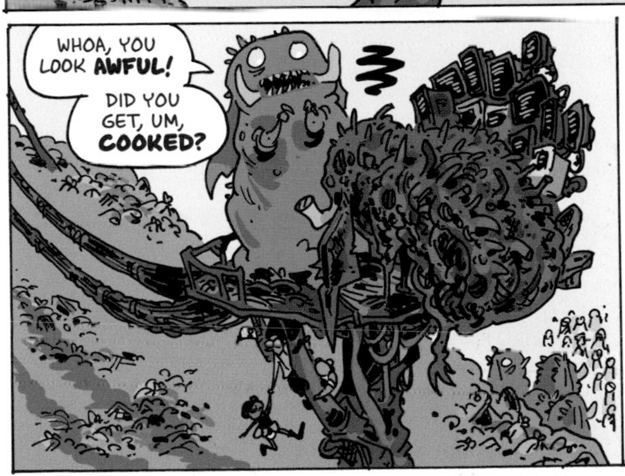

NOW GET DOWN THERE AND HELP SHORE UP THE PERIMETER. WE DON'T WANT HUMANS **ESCAPING** WHEN THE FEAST STARTS.
OKAY, I'M GOING. UM, HOPE YOU FEEL BETTER SOON. **OUCH.**

TAP TAPPITY TAP
WHAT NOW?
I'M GOING TO BUY YOU SOME TIME ON THOSE COMPUTERS...

TAP
...MAKE IT **COUNT!**

TAP TAPPITY
TAP
TAP

DEEP BREATH

HEY, SPOT!

UNGH.
HAVEN'T YOU CAUSED ME **ENOUGH** TROUBLE TODAY?
TAP TAP
TAP
BEAT IT. SCRAM.
TAP TAP TAPPITY TAP TAP

I'M RIGHT HERE, TROLL! IN YOUR VERY **LAIR!**
DON'T YOU WANT TO **EAT ME?**

I **WANTED** TO EAT THAT NUT IN THE WHEELCHAIR, AND LOOK WHERE **THAT** GOT ME.
LEAVE ME ALONE, MEATBALL. I'VE GOT WORK TO DO.
TAP

YEAH, WE KNOW **ALL ABOUT** YOUR **"WORK."**
YOU'VE TAKEN OVER TATTLER AND YOU'RE USING IT TO STRESS PEOPLE OUT AND TRICK THEM INTO COMING HERE!
WE DIDN'T "TAKE OVER" **ANYTHING.**
TAP TAP

TATTLER WAS **OUR CREATION.**

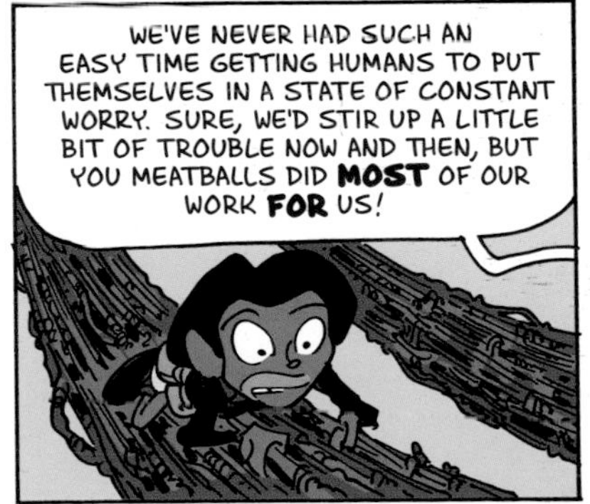
WE'VE NEVER HAD SUCH AN EASY TIME GETTING HUMANS TO PUT THEMSELVES IN A STATE OF CONSTANT WORRY. SURE, WE'D STIR UP A LITTLE BIT OF TROUBLE NOW AND THEN, BUT YOU MEATBALLS DID **MOST** OF OUR WORK **FOR** US!

WE'D MAKE UP THE MOST LUDICROUS "NEWS," AND YOU DELICIOUS, FOOLISH CREATURES WOULD SPREAD IT LIKE WILDFIRE!
PRACTICALLY **NO ONE** EVER **CHECKED** TO SEE IF WHAT THEY WERE SHARING WAS **TRUE.** YOU PLAYED RIGHT INTO OUR CLAWS!

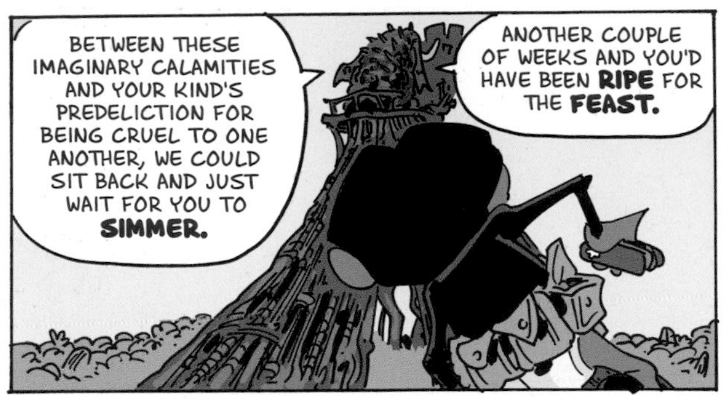
BETWEEN THESE IMAGINARY CALAMITIES AND YOUR KIND'S PREDELICTION FOR BEING CRUEL TO ONE ANOTHER, WE COULD SIT BACK AND JUST WAIT FOR YOU TO **SIMMER.**
ANOTHER COUPLE OF WEEKS AND YOU'D HAVE BEEN **RIPE** FOR THE **FEAST.**

WE'VE **NEVER** HAD SO MUCH **LEISURE TIME!**
I EVEN HAD A **VACATION NEST** BY THE **WATERFRONT.**

BUT **NOW** WE'RE IN **OVERDRIVE.** WE'VE GOT TO AMP EVERYONE'S STRESS UP AS FAST AND AS HIGH AS WE CAN. NOT THE **BEST** WAY OF PREPPING THE FOOD, BUT IT'S BETTER THAN NOTHING.

LIKE MICROWAVING SOMETHING THAT SHOULD BE SLOW-ROASTED—
HEY!
WHAT ARE YOU DOING?!

I'M CUTTING THESE CABLES. FIGURE THEY'RE WHAT'S CARRYING YOUR COMMANDS TO THE ANTENNAS AND STUFF.
WELL, **STOP IT!**

NO WAY, BARBECUE.
YOU WANT ME TO STOP, YOU'RE GONNA HAVE TO **MAKE ME.**
YOU WANT ME TO EAT YOU?
FINE.
I'LL EAT YOU.

CONSIDER YOURSELF A **POWER SNACK.** A LITTLE BOOST OF ENERGY TO HELP ME FOCUS ON THE TASK AT HAND.

HURRY, CAROL!

SERIOUSLY, QUIT CUTTING THE CABLES!

GUYS, THIS IS BAD.
I THINK THEY CREATED THEIR **OWN** OPERATING SYSTEM FROM SCRATCH, AND EVERYTHING'S WRITTEN IN **RUNES.**

I COULDN'T LOOK UP **MOVIE TIMES** WITH THIS SETUP, MUCH LESS **HACK IT.**
WE'LL DO THE NEXT BEST THING, THEN.

COME ON!
LET'S GET TOSSIN'!

YOU HAVE GOT TO BE **KIDDING** ME.

YOU MEATBALLS ARE **CRAZY**, DO YOU KNOW THAT?
I'M GONNA TEAR YOU TO **PIECES!**

WHOA!
SNAP
SNAP
SNAP
SNAP
SNAP

WHAA!

SNAPSNAP
SNAP

IT'S COMIN' DOWN!

OOF!
YOU KIDS ARE GOING TO **PAY** FOR THIS!

YOU THOUGHT **BEING EATEN** WOULD BE BAD?

THE THINGS I'M GOING TO—
...
UH-OH.

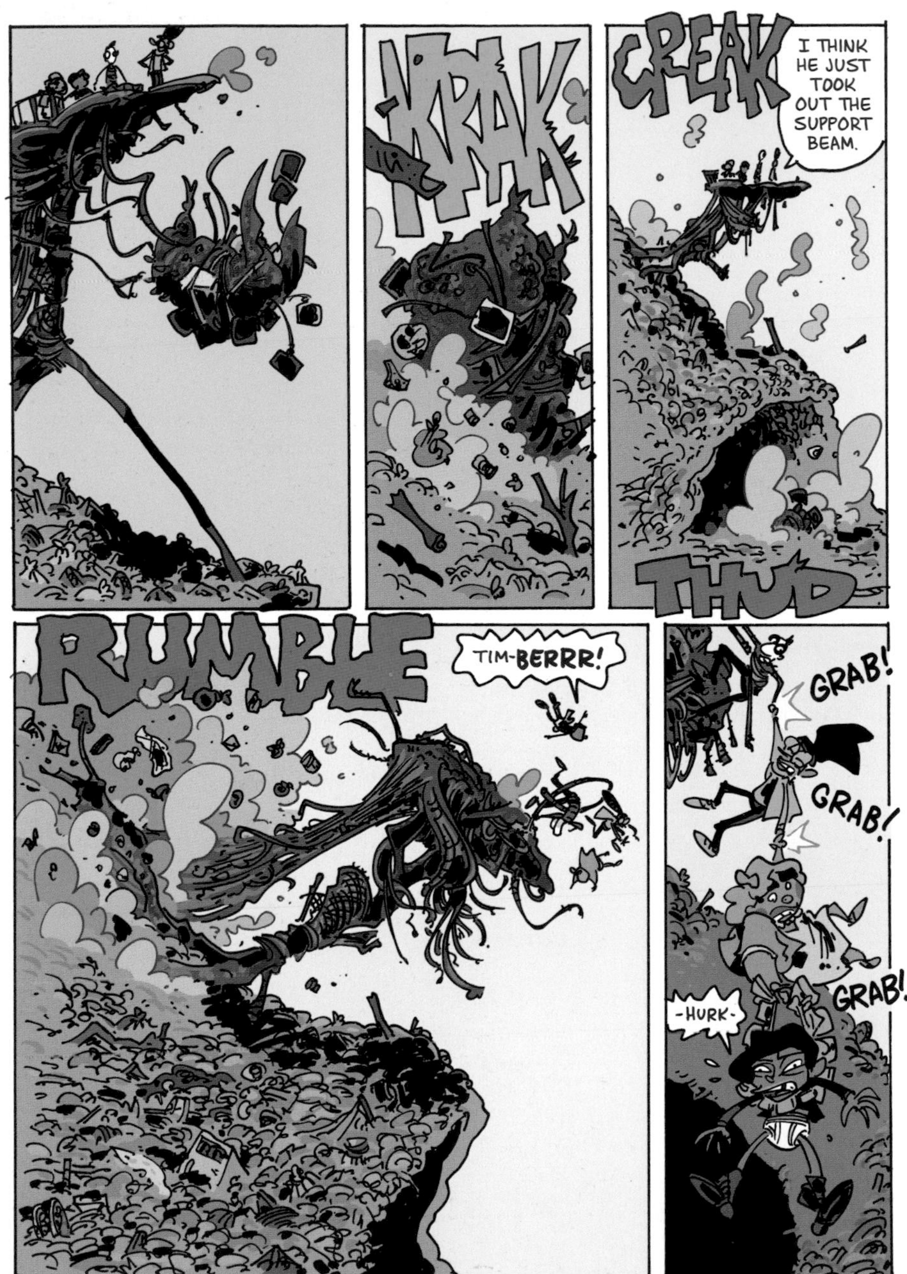
KRAK
CREAK
I THINK HE JUST TOOK OUT THE SUPPORT BEAM.
THUD
RUMBLE
TIM-BERRR!
GRAB!
GRAB!
GRAB!
-HURK-

CAN YOU CLIMB UP?
NO, I CAN BARELY HOLD ON!

BOOP BEE BEEP
OH, SHOOT. THAT'S MY MOM'S MESSAGE TONE.
GUESS WE KNOCKED OUT WHATEVER WAS JAMMING THE SIGNALS.
GUYS...

...I THINK WE'VE GOT A BIGGER PROBLEM THAN GRAVITY.
THE REST OF THE TROLLS HAVE NOTICED US.

OH, YOU DON'T HAVE TO WORRY ABOUT THEM.

YOU HAVE TO WORRY ABOUT ME.

THE KING HAS EMERGED!
ALL HAIL THE **TROLL KING!**

THOSE KIDS HAVE BEEN CAUSING TROUBLE FOR US ALL DAY.

I THINK **YOU'VE** BEEN THE CAUSE OF MOST OF OUR TROUBLES TODAY, OLD FRIEND.
FIRST YOU START THE CYCLE **EARLY,** THEN YOU WASTE PRECIOUS TIME AND TROLLPOWER TRYING TO FINISH OFF THAT TROLLFIGHTER.

YOU'VE BEEN GIVEN A LOT OF CHANCES BECAUSE YOU'VE SHOWN A TALENT FOR USING THE COMPUTERS TO MANIPULATE THESE HUMANS...

...BUT WITH THE TOWER LINES SEVERED, WE CAN'T CONTROL THE COMMUNICATION SIGNAL.

SO WHAT USE ARE YOU **NOW?**

WHAM

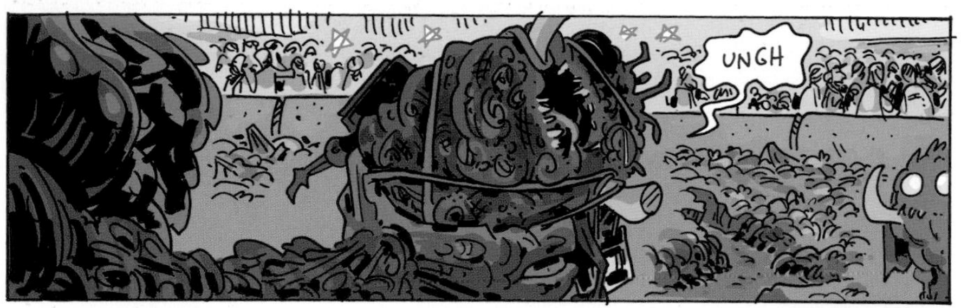
UNGH

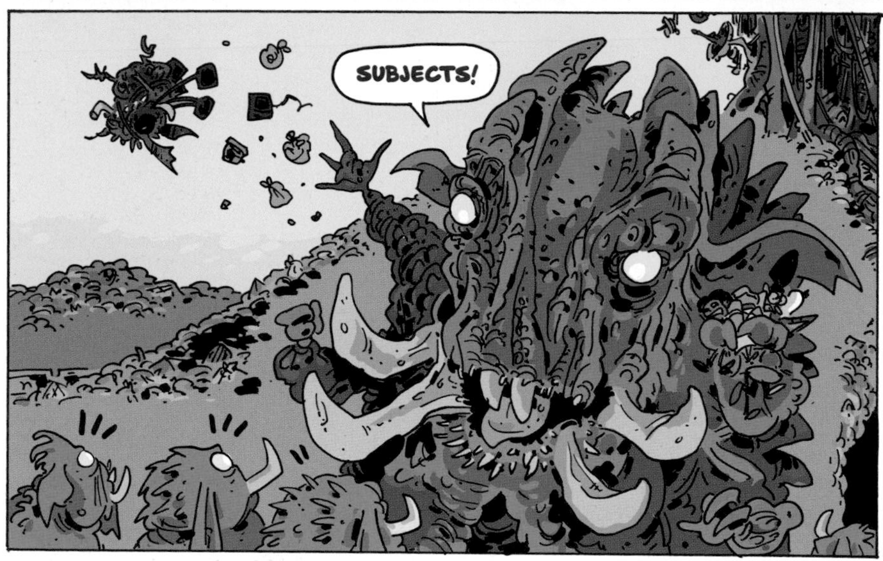
SUBJECTS!

OUR USURPATION OF THE HUMANS' COMMUNICATIONS SIGNAL HAS BEEN COMPROMISED.
THEY'RE ALL RECEIVING **CALLS** AND **MESSAGES.** SOON THEY'LL DISCOVER THAT THEY NEED NOT BE HERE, AND THEY'LL ATTEMPT TO **LEAVE.**

SO, CAN WE, UM, **EAT** THEM NOW?
SECURE ALL OF THE **EXITS** FIRST! THESE HUMANS HAVEN'T MARINATED LONG ENOUGH, SO WE MUST MAKE UP FOR THE MEAGER HORMONE LEVELS BY **GORGING OURSELVES** ON AS **MANY** AS **POSSIBLE!**

WE DON'T WANT THEM TO **PANIC** AND TRY TO **ESCAPE** BEFORE THEY'RE **PENNED IN...**
...BUT WE NEEDN'T WORRY ABOUT **THAT** WITH **YOU,** DO WE?

YOU WE CAN EAT **RIGHT NOW.**
ERRK!

SLURP
OH, THAT IS **SO GROSS.**

WHY ARE YOU CREEPS ROLLING AROUND IN THE **GARBAGE?**

WE'RE FIGHTING A GIANT TROLL IN AN EFFORT TO SAVE AS MANY PEOPLE AS WE CAN FROM BEING EATEN.
RUN, MADISON! SAVE YOURSELF!
GIVE IT A **REST,** CREEPS!

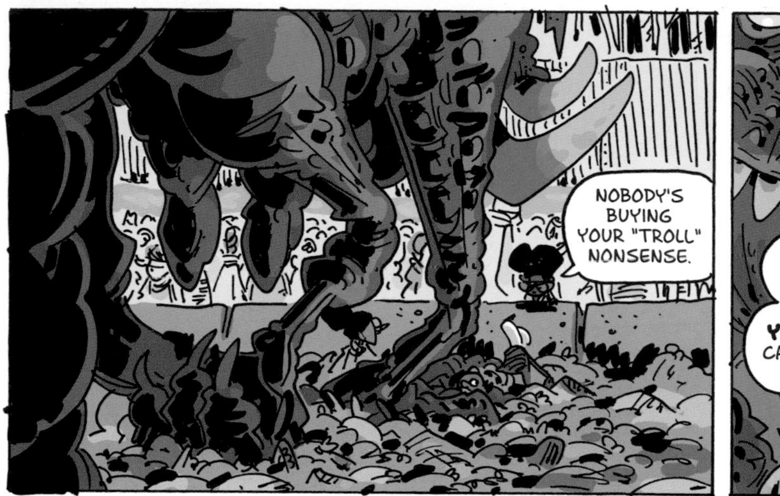

THE ONLY THING **I** SEE IS THIS E-MAIL FROM MY COUSIN THAT FINALLY CAME THROUGH.

WHAT'S THIS? THERE'S A VIDEO FILE ATTACHED?

WELL, WELL, WELL! IT LOOKS LIKE MY COUSIN **SAVED** THE VIDEO OF ROSARIO SINGING **BEFORE** CAROL TOOK IT OFFLINE!

NOTHING'S GONNA STOP ME FROM BEING A PRINCESS

ROAR
NOTHING'S GONNA STOP ME FROM BEING A PRINCESS

SOME MAY POINT AND SOME MAY SCOFF
TURN THAT **HORRIBLE** NOISE **OFF!**

BUT I WILL ONLY SHAKE IT OFF
NOTHING'S GON—

CRNCH

DID YOU GUYS SERIOUSLY JUST BREAK MY PHONE?!
YOU ARE GONNA BE IN **SO MUCH TROUBLE!**
EVEN A HIDEOUS MONSTER CAN'T STAND MY SINGING!
AWW, WHAT DOES **HE** KNOW?

SURE, MAYBE YOU'RE A LITTLE **WARBLY,** BUT—
SHH!

OH, MAN, THAT WAS **AWFUL!**

YOU ALL RIGHT, YOUR MAJESTY?
YEAH, YEAH. BUT THOSE DANG KIDS SKITTERED OFF WHILE I WAS **DISTRACTED.**

IS THE PERIMETER SECURE YET?
ALMOST, SIR!

A FEW MORE TROLLS ARE MOVING INTO PLACE ALONG THE SOUTHERN WALL.
IN A COUPLE OF MINUTES THE HUMANS WILL HAVE NO WAY TO ESCAPE, AND WE CAN **CHOW DOWN!**

A COUPLE OF MINUTES? WE'RE DOOMED! **EVERYBODY'S** DOOMED!
WE **MIGHT** STILL HAVE A **CHANCE.**

NOW THAT I CAN GET ONLINE AGAIN, I LOOKED UP "TRILL."
IT MEANS A SERIES OF BOUNCING MUSICAL NOTES.

"A TRILL FROM PASSION'S FOUNTAINHEAD DECLARE..."
"...FOR **STRAIN BELIEVED** IS MORE THAN IT CAN BEAR."
"STRAIN" CAN MEAN A PASSAGE OF **MUSIC.**

SO **MUSIC** IS OUR WEAPON AGAINST THE TROLLS?
SEE, ROSARIO, YOUR SINGING ISN'T SO BAD! **ANY** SONG WILL HURT THEM!
NO. NOT JUST **ANY** SONG.
IT HAS TO BE A SONG THAT THE SINGER IS **PASSIONATE** ABOUT.
A SONG THE SINGER **BELIEVES IN,** WITH ALL OF HIS OR HER **HEART.**

LIKE WHEN ROSARIO SINGS "NOTHING'S GONNA STOP ME FROM BEING A PRINCESS."

OH, NO. NONONONONO.

ROSARIO, YOU **HAVE** TO!
NO WAY!

I WOULD **DIE** BEFORE I'D **SING** IN **PUBLIC.**
AND GIVEN THE SITUATION, I CLEARLY MEAN THAT LITERALLY.
OH, JEEZ, I THINK I'M HYPERVENTILATING.

THERE'S
—GASP—
THERE'S GOT TO BE SOMETHING **ELSE** WE CAN DO!
YOU'RE **IT,** ROSARIO. WE'VE ONLY GOT SECONDS LEFT.
AND IT'S NOT JUST **YOU** WHO WILL DIE IF YOU DON'T SING.
IT'S **ALL** OF THESE **PEOPLE.**

...
WHAUGH!
I'M SORRY.
I CAN'T.
I **JUST CAN'T.**

IT'S **OKAY,** ROSARIO.

AREN'T...
AREN'T YOU GUYS **MAD** AT ME?
NOT EVEN A LITTLE.
ROSARIO, YOU FIGHT HARDER FOR YOUR FRIENDS THAN ANYONE, AND YOU HAVE **NEVER LET US DOWN.**
IF YOU SAY YOU CAN'T SING, WE **BELIEVE** YOU.

EVERYBODY HAS LIMITS TO WHAT THEY CAN DO, ROSARIO.

EVEN PRINCESSES.

ALL OF MY DAYS I'VE BEEN SHUT AWAY

AFRAID TO FAAAAAAACE THE WORLD

WHAT WILL THEY CRY WHEN THEY SEE THAT I
AM JUST A LONELY FRIGHTENED GIRL
HEY, LOOK, EVERYBODY!

IT'S THAT SINGING KID FROM THE VIDEO!

WELL, GO ON, KID. SING YOUR SONG!
YEAH, ROSARIO...

...SING YOUR SONG.

MY FAITHFUL TROLLS!
THE FEASTING IS AT HAND!

EAT YOUR **FILL,** AND LET NOT A SINGLE HUMAN **ESCA—**
MY TIIIIIME IS NOOOOOWWW

I'LL CLAIM MY PLACE
I'LL HOLD MY FACE UP HIGH

NOTHING'S GONNA STOP ME FROM BEING A PRINCESS
NOTHING'S GONNA STOP ME FROM BEING A PRINCESS
RRAWR! MAKE IT STOP!

THIS IS HILARIOUS!
SHE'S TERRIBLE!
SHH!
IT'S THAT GIRL FROM THE VIDEO!
SOME MAY POINT AND SOME MAY SCOFF
BUT I WILL ONLY SHAKE IT OFF

THAT KID'S ALL OVER THE PLACE PITCH-WISE, BUT SHE SURE IS ENTHUSIASTIC.
IT'S ADORABLE. IT REMINDS ME OF WHEN THE KIDS USED TO SING AROUND THE HOUSE.
NOTHING'S GONNA STOP ME FROM BEEEING...

SOMEONE EAT THAT GIRL!
NOW!

RAWRR

...MEEEEEE!

WOW.
KEEP SINGING, ROSARIO!
HA HA HA
YEAH, KEEP SINGING!
GET HER! I COMMAND IT!

IF THOSE TROLLS TEAR INTO THE CROWD TRYING TO GET ROSARIO, THEY'LL HURT A LOT OF PEOPLE.
COME ON!
AND **KEEP SINGING!**
I MIGHT BE SHY BUT IT'S TIME THAT I
THROW CAUTION TOOOO THE WIND

DON'T **COWER! ATTACK!**
THERE IS NO CROWD
WHERE I WON'T BE PROUD...
INTO THE LION'S DEN!

...TO LET THAT PRINCESS DEEP WITHIN...
HEY, IT DOESN'T HURT!
YOU'RE RIGHT!

KINDA PITCHY, THOUGH.
ROSARIO, IT ISN'T WORKING!
SING LOUDER!
IT'S NOT THE **VOLUME,** IT'S THE **CONVICTION!**

YOU HAVE TO **BELIEVE** WHAT YOU'RE SINGING. **THINK** ABOUT THE WORDS! **FEEL** THEM!
...SHINE LIKE A BEACON
FINALLY WE CAN
GET WHERE WE NEED TO **GOOOOOOOOO**
ROAR
OH, NO.
IT HURTS AGAIN.

CONFIDENT, STRONG
HERE'S WHERE I BELONG

LET EVERYBODY
KNOOOW

MY
TIIIIME
IS
NOOOW

I'LL TAKE MY CROWN

I'LL STAND UP PROOOUD AND TALL

NOTHING'S GONNA STOP ME FROM BEING A PRINCESS
NOTHING'S GONNA STOP ME FROM BEING A PRINCESS
SING IT, SISTER!
STOP, YOU'RE AWFUL!
AWESOME!

I MAY SOAR OR I MAY FALL
BUT EITHER WAY I'LL GIVE MY ALL
RAWRRR!
I WILL NOT BE DEFEATED BY A CHILD!
ROAR!
CRASH

YOU MONSTROUS LITTLE BEAST!
MY WHOLE CLAN HAS BEEN WIPED OUT BY YOUR CONTEMPTIBLE YODEL!
WHY'D SHE STOP?
MAYBE THE FALLING OVER IS PART OF THE PERFORMANCE.
PCHS

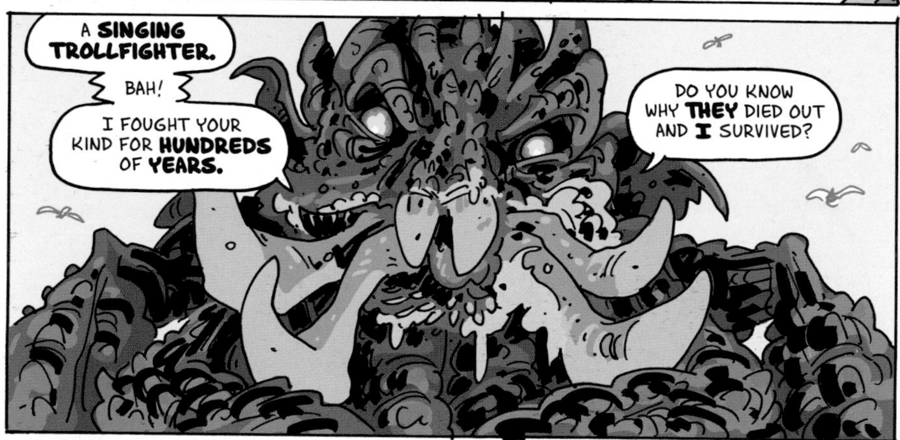
A SINGING TROLLFIGHTER.
BAH!
I FOUGHT YOUR KIND FOR HUNDREDS OF YEARS.
DO YOU KNOW WHY THEY DIED OUT AND I SURVIVED?

BECAUSE WHEN ALL THE CHIPS ARE DOWN...
...NONE OF YOU REALLY BELIEVE WHAT YOU SING.

YOU KNOW IN YOUR HEART THAT IT DOESN'T REALLY HAVE THE POWER TO DESTROY ME, BECAUSE YOU KNOW IN YOUR HEART THAT YOU DOUBT YOUR SONG.

THE TROLLFIGHTERS OF OLD SANG SONGS ABOUT KILLING TROLLS, AND USED THEM TO DO SO! BUT YOU?

YOU SING A CHILDISH ANTHEM ABOUT BEING BRAVE.
ABOUT BEING PROUD OF YOURSELF NO MATTER WHAT.

YOU'RE NOT PROUD OF YOURSELF. YOU'RE ASHAMED. AND YOU SHOULD BE!

I CAN'T BELIEVE YOU'D HAVE THE GALL TO ASSAULT THESE PEOPLE WITH YOUR TERRIBLE, AMATEURISH WARBLING!
DIDN'T YOU HEAR THEM LAUGHING AT YOU? DIDN'T YOU HEAR THEIR SCORN?

NOTHING HAS TO STOP YOU FROM "BEING A PRINCESS," BECAUSE YOU'RE ALREADY AS FAR FROM BEING A PRINCESS AS ANY HUMAN COULD BE!
LEAVE HER ALONE!

THUD

YOU'RE JUST A FRUMPY LITTLE WEIRDO IN A GARBAGE-STAINED SWEATERSET WITH A TERRIBLE SINGING VOICE...

...AND YOUR SONG
MEANS
NOTHING.

GRAB!

I **AM** A FRUMPY LITTLE WEIRDO.
SO ANY SONG THAT MAKES ME FEEL LIKE I'M **NOT** ONE...

...MEANS **EVERYTHING.**

NOTHING'S GONNA STOP ME FROM BEIIIIING...

MEEEE!

OW!
THUD

NOT TOO BAD, KID.
THANKS.

ROSARIO, THAT WAS **AMAZING!**
GOOD THING THAT TROLL KING TOOK THE TIME TO TRY AND MAKE YOU FEEL BAD ABOUT YOURSELF INSTEAD OF JUST STUFFING YOU DOWN HIS GULLET.
I WAS WONDERING ABOUT THAT WHILE HE WAS **DOING** IT, AND I HAVE A **HYPOTHESIS.**

HE HAD ALREADY **HEARD** ROSARIO'S SONG WHEN IT WAS DESTROYING THE **OTHER** TROLLS. I THINK IT WAS DESTROYING HIM, TOO, BUT SINCE HE WAS BIGGER OR OLDER OR WHATEVER, IT WAS TAKING LONGER TO HURT HIM.

MAYBE GETTING YOU TO STOP **BELIEVING** IN YOUR **SONG** WOULD STOP IT FROM **DESTROYING** HIM. LIKE TAKING AN ANTIDOTE AFTER DRINKING POISON!

THAT WOULD EXPLAIN HOW HE WAS ABLE TO SURVIVE HIS BATTLES WITH THE FIRST TROLLFIGHTERS, THE SINGING ONES, CENTURIES AGO.
OR HE WAS JUST A GRADE-A **JERK** WHO LIKED MAKING PEOPLE **FEEL BAD!**

OR HE WAS JUST A GRADE-A JERK WHO LIKED MAKING PEOPLE FEEL BAD.
SO EVERYONE IS SAFE? ALL OF THE TROLLS HAVE BEEN DESTROYED?
NOT **ALL.**
COME ON!

GERARD, YOU FOUND CLARA!
YOU WERE RIGHT, GUYS. THE TATTLER MESSAGES WERE FAKE.
DIDN'T SEE ANY "TROLLS," THOUGH.

WE **DID** SEE YOUR WEIRD "PERFORMANCE." THAT'S **EXACTLY** THE TYPE OF THING I SAID **NOT** TO DO!
THOUGH THAT PART WHERE YOU HOVERED IN THE AIR LOOKING ALL SAD **WAS** PRETTY ROCKSTAR.
I WASN'T HOVERING, I WAS BEING HELD UP BY AN INVISIBLE TROLL KING.
WHAT ARE WE LOOKING FOR, CAROL?
UP ON THE FENCE.

AT LEAST ONE TROLL SURVIVED...

ZZZ
...OUR OLD FRIEND **SPOT.**

ZZZ
SNORT
ZZZ
IS HE SLEEPING?
I THINK THE TROLL KING KNOCKED HIM OUT.

SPOT DIDN'T BLOW UP LIKE THE OTHERS BECAUSE HE WASN'T **AWAKE** TO HEAR ME **SING!**
ZZZ
MAN, HE IS **OUT.** IT LOOKS LIKE HE'S ALREADY IN THE HIBERNATION PHASE!
IT MIGHT BE YEARS BEFORE HE WAKES UP. DECADES, EVEN.

WELL, I CAN RIG UP A MOTION SENSOR THAT WE CAN STRAP TO HIM.
WHEN HE WAKES UP, WE'LL KNOW IT.
AND WE CAN COME DOWN HERE FROM TIME TO TIME TO STUDY HIS PHYSIOGNOMY. THIS'LL BE THE CREATURE COMPENDIUM'S MOST DETAILED AND ACCURATE ENTRY YET!
YOU KIDS GET DOWN FROM THERE!

THERE'S BROKEN GLASS, RUSTY METAL, AND WHO KNOWS **WHAT** KIND OF DANGEROUS STUFF UP THERE IN THAT GARBAGE.

SHERIFF OBIE...
YOU HAVE **NO IDEA.**

DON'T WORRY, BOSS. THAT STUFF ISN'T GOING ANYWHERE.

DO YOU THINK WE SHOULD TELL THEM THA—

NO. NO, WE SHOULD NOT.

Z

THE END

ABOUT THE AUTHOR

Chris Schweizer has never seen a ghost, but he's worked in three places that were supposed to be haunted: an old restaurant, an old mental hospital, and an old hotel. When he was in college, he lived in a house that *The Week* magazine later called "The Most Haunted Place in England."

Chris has been a college professor, a hotel manager, a movie theater projectionist, a guard at a mental hospital, a martial arts instructor, a set builder, a church music leader, a process server, a life-drawing model, a bartender, a car wash attendant, a bagboy, a delivery boy, a choirboy, a lawn boy, a sixth-grade social studies teacher, a janitor, a speakeasy proprietor, a video store clerk, a field hand, a deckhand, a puppeteer for a children's television show, a muralist, a kickboxer, and a line worker at a pancake mix factory. He likes being a cartoonist best. He lives in Kentucky with his wife and daughter.